Adrift in the universe. . . .

With their home planet destroyed, they had to find a new world on which to live, for they could not survive on their starship forever.

But every alien planet that the colonists thought might be promising turned out to be lethal, implacably hostile to life. One was a mass of automatic defense systems programmed to annihilate any intruder—defense systems whose alien architects had long since withered into racial oblivion. Another world seemed like a paradise, until colonists began falling down dead, killed by weapons that no one could imagine.

On and on they voyaged through space. Would they ever find a new world on which to survive?

". . . a very skillful dramatic rendering . . ."
—Library Journal

AND ALL THE STARS A STAGE

JAMES BLISH

AVON
PUBLISHERS OF BARD, CAMELOT AND DISCUS BOOKS

A somewhat abridged version of this novel first appeared in
AMAZING SCIENCE FICTION STORIES, Vol. 34, Nos. 6
and 7, June and July 1960; that version Copyright © 1960 by
Ziff-Davis Publishing Company.

AVON BOOKS
A division of
The Hearst Corporation
959 Eighth Avenue
New York, New York 10019

First Avon Printing, May, 1974.
Fourth Printing.

Printed in the U.S.A.

To Robert and Barbara Silverberg

1

It had all begun, Jorn Birn thought dispiritedly, with the exploding star.

The thought did not cheer him much. It is a hard thing to have to blame one's troubles upon an event which took place three hundred years ago, particularly when one's troubles are present, immediate, and full of nagging little details which seem to have nothing to do with history at all—let alone with so remote a subject as astronomy.

Take for example the present instance. Given, to begin with, a young bachelor sitting alone in his government-allotted room in an all-male "residence conclave"—the government's totally transparent euphemism for a barracks or dormitory, combining only the grimmer features of each. Given, secondly, the morning television newscast, with its usual quota of stories which seemed to differ from day to day but actually were always the same: the swearing-in of the first World Legislature to be composed entirely of women delegates; the failure (again) to meet the year's food production quota, despite the most intensive, back-

breaking exploitations of hydroponics, undersea farm-
ing, cloud culture, desert irrigation, deep-tank mass
cell culture and half a dozen other techniques the
names of which conveyed absolutely nothing to Jorn;
the successful landing of a robot-probe expedition on
the tiny, sunbaked, and intransigently useless planet
nearest the Sun, whose name fled out of Jorn's head
as slipperily as it had skidded in on the oil of the newscaster's voice; the verdict in a sensation trial involving
a minor government functionary who had brought a
paternity suit against someone in her official *familias*
—sensational only in that the usually conclusive blood
tests having failed for some complicated genetic reason, she seemed to want to *establish* paternity, rather
than to disavow it and thus take the child into her
own crêche (and two seconds after he had heard the
verdict, Jorn could not remember whether she had
won or lost, and could think of no reason why he
should care).

And given, finally, the spectacle of an unusually
intelligent young man, still almost fully in possession
of the standard engineer's education of his time, des-
perately sitting through this barrage of unchangingly
insignificant news stories, as daily and as interchange-
able as a dish of catmeat, in the sole hope of hearing
something which might lead him to a job. Of course
a television newscast is a wholly inappropriate medium
in which to run a Help Wanted column, since the
listener cannot decide whether or not he is interested
in a given bid until he has heard it all, by which time
it is too late for him to write down the address and
the telephone number and such other details as he
may need to study or to carry out onto the beltways
with him. Employers who were really seriously in
search of skilled help invariably still resorted to the
newspapers, and in the very rare cases where they also

inserted a television appeal, they took it for granted that anyone in whom they were likely to be interested would be making a telefax transcript of the entire job-openings announcement. This was nonsensical, since nobody but an unmarried male would be desperate enough to hope to locate a job through these television announcements in the first place, and the sets in the residence conclave rooms did not include telefax equipment; it was of course true that the set in the recreation hall had a telefax attachment, but no bachelor in his right mind could hope to compete with two hundred others for that single sheet of blurrily printed brown paper, which even when new looked as though it had been rescued almost too late from a fire, and still have any time left over for tracking down the very few jobs it announced. If you had hoped to have a hearing at all, you had to hop, the moment you got the word. You couldn't afford to waste time hanging around the orifice of a community telefax, until it should choose—as it did only once an hour—to protrude the long sickly brown tongue of its transcript.

All this was difficult enough to blame upon a star that had exploded three hundred years ago; but in view of the persistent triviality of the news, and the high unlikelihood that the job-opportunities commercial could offer anything whatsoever worth pounding the beltways to get, Jorn managed. In a world in which hardly anything satisfied him, it was easy enough to wonder how today might have differed from itself if history could somehow have been re-arranged; and the exploding star was a natural beginning to such a daydream, since before that event nothing, really, could be said to have happened at all.

Oh, there had been the usual wars, the usual pestilences, the usual migrations, the usual births and declines of nations, but the details of daily life for the ordinary human being hardly changed from age to age. The industrial revolution, of course, overturned all that; in the short course of slightly more than a century, the average citizen of the wealthier countries found himself in possession of riches beyond even the dreams of kings of any earlier time; but even that great event was dwarfed by the supernova. In fact, if Jorn remembered correctly, the industrial revolution had been still in progress when the star exploded, though how far along it had progressed he could not be sure—his historical daydreams being more than a little impeded by the fact that history had always been his weakest subject; the might-have-beens kept getting mixed up with the facts.

In any event, when that mighty star rose in the night, everything was changed. For a week it grew brighter and brighter, until it far outshone any other object in the sky but the sun. At the peak of its 55-day life, it was clearly visible in the daytime, a spearpoint of light too intense to be looked at directly. At night, it cast distinct shadows and indeed was more than bright enough to read by, so that for a little while the night as everyone had known it in all the centuries before was effectively abolished.

Thereafter it waned, slowly. It was still there, and could still be seen by the naked eye if one knew where to look: a dim, ghostly blob of light, like a flower in a medieval field of uncut grass, of about the eighth magnitude. Through the telescope it was a spreading, crawling cloud of incandescent gas something under two light years in diameter, vaguely crablike in shape, still expanding in the sky at the rate of about four angular seconds per year. Its apparent diameter was already so great that a half-credit coin held at arm's length would not quite cover it, although of course the nebula itself was quite invisible to the naked eye.

There was still a star in its heart, but it was a shrunken corpse now, well on its way toward becoming a white dwarf.

But the naked eye had not been the only observer even then. By an amazing stroke of luck—bad luck, in Jorn's soured view—one of history's greatest astronomical theorists had been watching it, through one of history's first really efficient large electronically amplified telescopes, at the instant it had exploded. Since it proved to be located in a thin dust cloud, undetected until then, the expanding globe of light racing outward from its first brightening afforded a direct visual check of the speed of light, in the vastest laboratory imaginable; while successive spectrographs of the entire cataclysm unveiled the secrets of not just one, but a whole series of nuclear reactions, several of which proved to be duplicatible—with considerable effort—on a controllable scale. The Age of Power had arrived, borne upon starlight.

A head poked around the door into Jorn's ruminations.

"Got the news on?" it said. "Who's ahead?"

It was Jurg Wester, a fellow resident; Jorn was not particularly fond of him, but a prudent man did not invite animosity in quarters as close and lacking in privacy as a conclave. Today he was looking unusually seedy; his state-issue suit looked as though it might have been slept in. But then, they all got to looking like that after a while; the fabric wrinkled readily and getting the wrinkles pressed out was too expensive for a bachelor to undertake very often—too expensive, and mostly too purposeless.

"The women, who else?" Jorn said. "Sit down and shut up a minute, Jurg. I want to hear this."

"You want a job shoveling garbage?" Jurg said, but he subsided after that accommodatingly enough, his eyes slowly glazing as he watched the screen. Jorn, only a little distracted, did not find it difficult to recapture the skein of his musings.

For the Age of Woman had indeed followed almost directly upon the Age of Power, though nobody had accurately foreseen it at the time. Probably such a prophet, had he existed, would not have been heeded anyhow. The relevant technique was called sperm electrophoresis, a ridiculously simple trick to perform in glassware—and the pharmaceutical manufacturers had quickly come up with a medium, an anion or cation exchange gel, which made it equally easy to perform *in situ*. Its purpose was sex determination of the child at conception.

By hindsight, Jorn thought gloomily, it ought to have been realized that the first several generations to have the trick made available to them would respond by "starting with a boy." That preference had already existed, and indeed was so primitive that it might possibly be instinctual. The result, in any event, was the world of today, heavily overburdened with males, most of them useless—at least in the sense that neither the economy nor the society could find places for most of them.

Being a man, Jorn was inclined to think that the real death blow had been struck by the release of Selektrojel to the populace as an over-the-counter or nonprescription item. Possibly if its use had been restricted to couples psychiatrically certified to *need* a baby of a given sex—like, say, a couple to whom unaided nature had given only a string of five daughters, or, no, better make it nine...But that would not have worked either. The demand for the stuff had been far too great. Like alcohol, the trade in it could be regulated more or less effectively but it could never be restricted in any meaningful sense.

All the same, Jorn was aware of his prejudices, and it was clear enough to him that radical changes in the social mores had been in the making even back then. Had it not been Selektrojel, it would have been something else. That had appeared almost simultaneously with another dangerous triumph of the pharmaceutical research laboratories: a cheap, simple, safe, foolproof oral contraceptive. This, coupled with the fact that venereal disease had disappeared (as a natural consequence of the virtually complete conquest of infectious disease by chemotherapy, immunology, and universal sanitation), might easily have destroyed the immemorial family system entirely, by making sexual relations so free of any unwanted consequence that they could hardly seem worth the price of a lifetime contract, especially to the innately roving-eyed male. ("In fact," one of the leading doctors of the time had remarked in an immortal burst of unconscious humor, "venereal disease is now almost as pleasant to cure as it is to catch.") Legal protection could still be afforded the woman afflicted with an accident of impulse, since modern genetics made it possible to determine the parents of any child ninety-nine times out of a hundred by blood tests alone.

That much *had* been predicted, by one of the most brilliant novelists of the period; but it had not worked out that way—not entirely—and for this Jorn had reluctantly to give the credit to Selektrojel. Sexual customs were indeed immensely less constrained now than they had been in the times of Jorn's grandparents, but the family had not been shattered. Being able to choose the sex of their children had given people enough of a stake in the family system to turn the tide in favor of retaining it. To be sure, the present prevalence of harems of male concubines, and the way women officeholders had of recruiting male staffs by marrying them—that was not yet official, but it would become so on the inevitable day when the first woman World Director was elected and chose her cabinet that way—would have stunned and revolted Jorn's grandparents, but it *was* still recognizably a family system...

...Which did Jorn Birn no good whatsoever. The fourth boy in his family—which, since his mother had been moderately well off, had provided him with three people to call "father"—he had been farmed out to a crêche not long after infancy, as a luxury his mother had decided she could no longer afford. He had been state-raised, state-educated, and state-supported ever since. Nor did he have any hope of marrying into some influential woman's staff, or indeed much hope of marrying at all; though he had never heard of Cinderella, he recognized the standard plot of the usual television drama for the opiate it was.

Engineering or no engineering, it sometimes seemed to him in his worst moments that he had no prospects but those of becoming a public gigolo. But he was invariably brought up short by the realization that he was not really attractive enough to make a living at it against the widespread competition; and in any event, his powers in this field were at the age of twenty-five not only unpracticed, but outright untested. Jorn Birn was simply a glut on the market, any market, and that was the end of the matter.

"And winds from the northeast, moderate to fresh," the newscaster was saying brightly. "And now, let's see what's stirring in the way of job opportunities. We have an unusual item to lead off with. And there's no use listening to *this* one, girls, because it's for a *man.*" There was an appreciative giggle. "Here's an outfit that says it wants a *young male* with technical training. It won't pay him much and he'll have to work long hours in all kinds of uncomfortable and dangerous situations. 'Death not unlikely,' it says here, 'but survivors *may* become *famous*.' Well, *well*. The address is room a-ten-prime, Research Tower, Central City. Here's a *big* chance, fellows—be the first man in history to circumnavigate the sun on skis, or something! And now, let's get down to *serious* business. Continental Atomics informs your communicator that it *urgently* needs five young women, in the twenty-to-forty age bracket, to administer a new power-conversion project. Although previous experience *is* preferred, the firm—"

Convulsively, Jorn switched the set off. That was that.

"But why'd you bother to write the address down?" Jurg said immediately. Jorn was startled; somehow, he had assumed that the other man had fallen asleep with his eyes open. "It's all klax anyhow, you ought to know that."

"I don't know. I do it by habit. And a good thing this time—she was so busy being funny, she forgot to repeat it."

"Klax," Jurg said firmly, and ran his index finger under his nose. "If that job's a good thing. I'm a town clock with sixteen chimes. The witch was right—it's a recruiting poster for one of those space medicine slaughterhouses. They'll squirt you off to an orbit a thousand miles out from nothing at all, record your blood pressure and a little muffled cussing by radio—and then, when they somehow don't manage to bring you back, they'll shed a tear and scratch your name onto some imperishable back fence with a blunt nail."

Jorn grinned in spite of himself. Jurg undoubtedly had hit the target pretty close to dead center: that item *had* had all the ring of a lure of some kind of space travel experiment, which was already no more than a nearly-standard way for a young man in despair to commit suicide... especially since the money involved, even if you did survive, was invariably less than the residence-conclave dole.

And yet, and yet... perhaps only because he had been observed writing the address down, perhaps only because he a little bit disliked Jurg's habitual air of knowing all the answers in advance, he felt himself turning stubborn.

"Maybe so," he said slowly. "But I've heard a lot of those ads. She said, 'Survivors may become famous'— I can't remember ever having heard that hook before, except when I was a little boy. It certainly doesn't sound like the lunar colony project, just to begin with."

"No," Jurg agreed, "there's too many people settled on that rock-ball already. It's just the usual guinea-piggery—a satellite, or maybe an interplanetary probe: tell us what you can see, old man, until we can't hear you any more, and then s-t-r-e-t-c-h that last can of cream-of-fungus-mycelium soup. Besides, why do you want to be famous, anyhow?"

"I don't, exactly," Jorn said, irritated. "But if it meant what it said... well, fame is negotiable, if you handle it right."

"How do you do that? By marrying the next World Director?"

"No. For that I'd have to be lovable, too—all the video shows tell you that, don't they? But being famous *might* help. A lot of women these days think a little about good genes before they decide who they're going to marry next. If you weren't born of a rich mother, or one with political connections, it couldn't hurt to have something else conspicuous in

your record—something that shows that you're pretty
good in your own right."

"Dream on," Jurg said. "That's how they got us in
this trap in the first place, and that's just how they
mean to keep us there. We aren't ever going to get
out of it by swallowing their little myths down whole,
I'll tell you that much."

"Well, tell me some more while you're on the plat-
form. How *are* we going to get out of it?"

"The time will come," Jurg said, a little portentously,
scratching under one armpit. "I don't think you're
really ripe for it yet, Birn. But you'll come around to
it on your own before long; I know the type. I just
hope it isn't too late by then."

"Suit yourself," Jorn said shortly. He had heard nonsense like that before, often enough to know approximately what it was supposed to mean. He looked at
the address again, and then at his two-credit state-
issue watch. What harm could it do to follow the item
up? After all, he had nothing else meaningful to do.
His choices were restricted to listening to Jurg become
more and more cryptic, throwing Jurg out and watching the next episode of "Pat's Other Jon," or sitting in
a park surreptitiously chucking gravel at the birds. A
choice between another day of despair . . . and room
a-10-prime, Research Tower, Central City.

"Excuse me," he said. "I think I'm going for a walk."

It was high summer at its worst outside. The massive blue-white supergiant sun, an undulating variable
with more than a hundred different overlapping periods, was at one of its thousands of possible peaks of
three or more cycles. It turned the air into an invisible
cauldron, which might at any moment boil up into a
storm, very possibly one too violent for Weather Con-

trol to cope with—there had been an increasing number of those in the last few years.

Nevertheless, Jorn elected to take the beltways. He was lucky enough to be in Central City to begin with; but also, he had bought three books this month, which had nearly wiped out his carfare budget.

The sensed threshold of violence in the weather forced his thoughts reluctantly back to Jurg Wester, and the vague rumors of revolution which Jurg had been attempting to float. Jorn had heard them before, and not always from Jurg; they came drifting through the residence conclaves as ominously and unpredictably as thunderheads. It was a minor cross to Jorn that he was still unable to take much stock in them.

He had, to be sure, every reason to believe that the vast sexual proletariat of the bachelors was bored and desperate enough to welcome almost any imaginable kind of trouble. It was not hard to suspect, too, that the husbands and concubines were just as unreconciled to the role of belonging to the inferior sex. Anyone seriously examining the change which had come over the statistics of crime in the last two generations would draw very much the same conclusion.

All the same, he could not bring himself to hope that any open conflict between the sexes—as opposed to the natural, buried, and eternal conflict—could end by changing society more than slightly. You could of course change human nature, since in the long run that meant nothing more than changing human behavior; that had been done over and over again, quite often by design. But the one thing you could not change was human needs. In any formal war between the sexes, the defections from both sides would in the end wipe out even the possibility that either side could win, exactly as an ancient play Jorn had been forced to read at school had devoted five acts to insisting.

Damn Jurg Wester; but still, it *was* a nice notion to daydream about on an afternoon of incipient thunder. At least it helped Jorn to ignore the fact that he was hopelessly stumping the beltways again, the pockets of his SI suit without enough credits in them to clink against each other.

The beltways were depressingly well populated with men of all ages. Those who looked to be about Jorn's age or younger were dressed in a wild variety of styles. Though the SI suit was predictably in the majority, even that was often modified enough to accommodate the one mandatory feature of all the current styles, an outlandishly stuffed and padded codpiece. Where the men involved had the money for it, the suits were replaced entirely by shadow-cloaks— fundamentally a cross between a tailored toga and a front-split kilt. This was made of a synthetic fabric which took permanent creases almost as well as paper did, and hence could be folded and pleated by its owner to his own taste, so that in motion it afforded frequent but not quite predictable glimpses of whatever good points he thought he had. Here and there, too, Jorn saw a man in the highly conservative "business" coverall which was this year's uniform for the prosperous homosexual, a far more powerful class among career women than any of the normals were; these he eyed with a malice he knew to be at least half envy, for he had long ago determined that he had been born without the talent. All in all, his sex was a colorful aggregate; and all in all, they made him want to spit.

A male revolution? No, Jurg was wrong; it wasn't likely. There were already too many different kinds

of males in the world, all intent upon maintaining
their differentness, and if possible, parlaying it into
the unique. They had suffered themselves to be
divided—and from now on, they would be ruled.

2

Room a-10-prime, Research Tower, Central City, was
an absolute madhouse.

It consisted primarily of a huge waiting room, almost
as big as a hall, most of which was fenced off from
the milling applicants. The fenced-in area was occupied by closely spaced desks where interviews were
conducted, or dictation given to standard government
vocoders. Outside the fence there was an oblong of
floor mostly taken up by massed ranks of folding
wooden chairs, like fugitives from a funeral. Here the
applicants sat waiting their turns to stand at one of
the writing banquettes along the wall and fill out a
limp, gray legal-length questionnaire which offered
not a single clue to what the victim was applying for.

Those who got past the first screening at the desk
by the gate, as Jorn eventually did, were transferred
to an interviewer; and if the interviewer was satisfied
—though "satisfied" was hardly the word, for the
young women who did the work somehow managed
to look as sour upon finding someone they could pass

as they did when (far more usually) they sent the
applicant ignominiously out—the legal-length form
was promptly reduced to a series of punches in three
stiff colored cards. The floor around the interviewing
desks was drifted over by the little red, yellow and
blue checks which had snowed down from the busily
snipping punches; they were also all over the tops of
the desks and even on the seats of the chairs. They
clung to the hair, settled into the creases of the SI
suits, became airborne at whim and floated up the
nose, and every so often, immediately following an
explosive sneeze, went flying in all directions toward
the ceiling like chaff through a silo. When this happened, the young woman interviewing the hapless
sneezer usually changed her expression from routine
disapproval to implacable grimness and sent him
packing, dropping his cards into the waste-can.

Jorn somehow managed to pass this test, though
still without learning anything at all about the job.
He was sent back to the ranked folding chairs to wait
while his cards were processed, with an enormous
roar which made all talk in the room impossible except
at a driving shout, by a computer which seemed to be
not so much analyzing the cards as chopping them
completely into more vari-colored little checks. After
more than an hour, during which the heat reduced
Jorn's SI suit to an assemblage of clinging dishrags
and the folding chair became increasingly impossible
to sit on comfortably regardless of how he tried to
accommodate himself to it, one of the young women
took a red card out of the stack in the computer's
return basket, stared at it with astonished disapproval,
and came to the rail to call Jorn's name. Simple
though it was, she had no difficulty in mispronouncing
it; obviously, she had had practice.

He was directed off the floor into a room not much

bigger than a closet, but which at least seemed to be air-conditioned. Here a middle-aged woman doctor asked him another hundred questions, these of such astonishing intimacy that he did not himself know the answers to nearly half of them. This, for some reason, seemed to satisfy her profoundly; he was told to step into the next room and take off all his clothes. Since the heat in the waiting room had long since converted the suit into a clammy, slowly disintegrating shroud, he was a little reluctant to do so, out of the conviction that he would never get it on again in one piece. Nevertheless he complied.

The disrobing awoke Tabath, his familiar, who raised her tiny crested head from his wrist to stare with unwinking yellow-eyed hostility at the glare and confusion. Though both glare and confusion were commonplace enough at the residence conclave, no one really yet knew how much the little basilisks learned from experience, even after nearly a century of studying them. Jorn was personally quite convinced that Tabath was unusually intelligent for a familiar, but he had the saving good sense to know that everyone thought well of their own—that bias was absolutely necessary in so personal a relationship, but that did not make it necessarily true.

The serpent shifted her two-foot length on his arm automatically and looked back up at Jorn. As usual, he had no idea what she wanted—as an ectoparasite she had no wants she needed to ask for—but the movement had the effect of making him notice that none of the naked men in the long line he was supposed to join was wearing a familiar.

As he hesitated, he heard behind him the clack-clack of sandals, and turned to see another woman doctor in the act of passing him. She was exceedingly striking, and somehow Jorn had the impression that he knew her. She was gray-haired, obviously old enough to be his grandmother, and yet at the same time quite beautiful—not with the hard gloss of the television actress, nor even that of the older woman fighting grimly to hold onto her looks, but with a soft feminine warmth which was as captivating as it was rare.

She stopped, apparently noticing his hesitation, and smiled at him quizzically.

"Don't worry," she said. "Just leave her with your clothes. She won't wander off and no one will bother her. You may have a *very* complete physical exam ahead of you, and we can't take the chance that she might misinterpret it."

That seemed logical enough. Jorn had never had an intensive physical before, and Tabath had been known to take even cursory ones as having aggressive intent. He began to stammer out his thanks, but the doctor had already smiled again and moved on. As he stared after her, he realized why it was that he had thought he knew her: She was Dr. Hary't Chase-Huebner, one of the world's foremost authorities in cancer research. He had seen her most recently on television only a month ago, in a newscast of the awarding of a government-sponsored prize.

Her presence here was convincing evidence that the job, whatever else it might prove to be, could hardly be what Jurg Wester had called "just the usual guinea-piggery"; but that was not the aspect of the encounter which impressed Jorn most. Instead, he was bemused to find that with a smile and a few words the scientist had cut right through his ritual dislike of women-in-general. In her own person she was a gentle but forcible reminder that women, like men, came in all colors of the personal spectrum: some bad, most indifferent, a few undeniably good. He found himself wondering how many husbands she had, and how much of her family she had kept with her past puberty; he remembered vaguely that she had a son—a son, no less!—who was an eminent physicist in his own right, with whom she occasionally collaborated on research problems which involved both sciences.

He sighed without being aware of it and stripped Tabath off his forearm. She promptly coiled fiercely around his hand, but by saying "Shower, Tabath" to her four or five times with increasing firmness, he managed to overcome her suspicions of the strange surroundings. Nevertheless, she promptly disappeared into one of his pockets; ordinarily she would have coiled inside his collar, where she could keep watch until he reappeared.

The first physical was relative superficial, strictly an assembly-line procedure. Once past it, however, Jorn found himself subject to an individual examination which more than justified Dr. Chase-Huebner's prophecy. He had never realized before that he had so many orifices worth looking into, so many internal organs to be palpated and X-rayed, so many body products worth sampling, so many vital processes recordable by appropriate machines. Had Tabath been present through all of this, she would indeed probably have bitten somebody—or, more likely, everybody. Even for Jorn it was something of an ordeal; when it was over, he felt as though he had just run a mile. (And he had in fact run about a quarter of that distance, on a treadmill, with a breathing mask over his nose and mouth.)

By this time he was deep into the labyrinth which was "room" a-10-prime, and had entirely lost sight and track of other applicants for the job, if indeed any other than himself had been allowed to penetrate this far. It had become wholly a private trial, in which he moved entirely alone through a strange universe where a new dragon lurked in every cave, unarmored, disweaponed and without even a familiar to share his defiance.

After the physical he was given a break for lunch. It was a better meal than he had been able to buy for himself at any time in his life, but his appreciation of it was somewhat dimmed by the company he was forced to eat it in—three specialists of some kind, one of them male and decidedly subordinate to the other two, who probed insistently for his opinions and his stores of information on a wide variety of subjects. So many of these questions were astronomical that they could not help but revive his Jurg-nurtured suspicions of space research; but others—those dealing with crop genetics, for instance, or the education of children—seemed wholly unrelated either to the astronomical questions or to each other.

The entire afternoon was given over to a battery of pencil-and-paper tests, all sufficiently difficult to prevent his finishing them in the allotted time ... all, that is, but one, wherein he discovered immediately that the questions were stacked in order of increasing difficulty, so that by tackling the last question first, he was able to speed up steadily and cross the wire with the answer to question number one just as the bell rang.

These consumed five hours, and he took them all nearly birthday-naked. He had been kindly supplied a sort of breech-clout or dhoti which prevented the many different chairs he had to sit in from tattooing his bottom indelibly, but that was all. When they were over, however, he was led back to his clothes and allowed to resume the terrified and nearly famished Tabath; she fairly leapt onto his arm, on which she found more than enough nervous perspiration to sate her hunger and make her grow half an inch in length in the bargain. To Jorn's consternation, however, his suit itself was immediately whisked away; he was given instead a tailored coverall of totally strange design. He was somewhat mollified to find that it fitted him far better than the suit ever had, and that it was of expensive material and fine workmanship; all the same it had so many pockets, zippers, tags, and attachments of odd location and unknown function—including many metal devices which looked for all the world like latch-staples—that even its undoubtable luxuriousness made him feel more nervous and outré than ever.

Then back into the labyrinth again, to a new room which proved instead to be a small but well-appointed apartment. Here he was given an excellent dinner; and, for a wonder, left for nearly three hours entirely to himself and—insofar as he could tell—unobserved. He was grateful; he had plenty to think about.

On the whole, though it had been a gruelling day, it had not been a bad one. At the very least it had seldom been dull, as most of his ordinary days were; he had been occupied every minute until now. Furthermore, he had gotten two first class meals out of it, and an expensive—though funny—new outfit (providing that they planned to let him keep it; that, of course, was not any too likely). And it had certainly all been novel; even if he failed to get the job, he could while away many a day to come with wondering what it could have been, playing with the manifold clues which had been heaped upon him today like pieces in the world's most mammoth cutout picture puzzle.

As the third hour progressed, however, he found himself first becoming gradually relaxed in spite of himself, and then imperceptibly crossing the line from there into restiveness. It was all very well to treat a superfluous male job applicant like a captive king, but he knew better than to suppose that it was being done out of pure nobility. There had to be a rationale behind this elaborate series of procedures; and now that he had been given the chance to recover his strength, his breath and his perspective, he felt an increasing urgency to get on with it. Even a labyrinth, after all, is supposed to have a heart—or at least, an exit.

Then there was a knock, and while he was still considering this unusual amenity, the door opened soundlessly. The young woman who came in could hardly have been any older than he was; in fact, though he was abominably poor at judging such matters—any woman with a reasonably competent or sophisticated manner usually struck him as being older than Jorn was—he thought she might well be younger. She was certainly very feminine; though she was wearing precisely the same outfit he was—evidently it was a kind of uniform—she filled it much more interestingly. After a moment's hesitation, he stood up.

"You're Jorn Birn," she said, looking up at him out of violet eyes with what he took to be a sort of automatic, impersonal appraisal. It did not really seem to be a question, but for want of any alternative, Jorn answered it anyhow.

"That's right."

"I hope you've finished your meal. If so, we can go now."

"I'm finished, thank you," Jorn said. "Go where?"

"To see the Director," she said, a little curtly. Evidently she was not used to being questioned by applicants. "We're ready for your interview."

"My interview!" Jorn exploded. Abruptly, he had

had more arrogance, impersonality and mystification than he could take. "What else have I been getting all day, anyhow?"

"Interviews, of a sort," she said coolly. "Naturally. Otherwise you would never have gotten this far. But now you're to talk to the Director—that's a different thing entirely."

"I see," Jorn said. "Meaning that I'm finally going to be told what it is that I'm applying for?"

"Obviously."

"If it were obvious to me, I wouldn't have asked," Jorn said. "However, lead on. After all, it *is* what I came here for."

As she turned, another thought occurred to him. "By the way," he said, "you know my name, but I'm afraid I didn't catch yours."

"I didn't offer it," she said. "And judging by your attitude, it's not likely that you're going to need it. I certainly hope not, anyhow. Come along."

He followed her out the door. On the whole he felt grimmer than ever.

"You don't make it sound as though it's up to you to decide," he said, a little maliciously.

At that she stopped in her tracks and swung on him. Her normally pretty face was drawn into an astonishing, unmistakable expression of pure disgust which left him speechless. He had long since become resigned to being rather unattractive, as well as superfluous; but somehow it had failed to occur to him that he might even be disgusting as well.

After an instant, however, she turned her back on him and resumed her march down the empty corridor.

"No," she said, in a light neutral voice which gave no hint of the spasm of emotion her face had just betrayed. "That's up to the Director."

The Director's room was seemingly in the innermost keep of the fortress that was room a-10-prime, but somehow it was light and airy all the same. Not greatly to Jorn's surprise, it was opulent as well, though its opulence was of a rather standardized sort: wooden desks instead of metal ones, chairs with dull red cushions instead of gray, a patternless carpet— also dull red—instead of a scuffed series of coats of rubber-base paint. There were five people there, not counting himself and the girl, among whom he recognized, with pleasure, only Dr. Hary't Chase-Huebner.

Very little of this, however, held his attention more than a moment. Thereafter he had eyes only for the Director.

The Director was a man.

"This would be Mr. Jorn Birn," the Director said, looking up from a fascicle of papers elaborately fastened inside a crimson folder. "Thank you, Ailiss; please sit down and join us. And Mr. Birn, please be seated there at the table. We're very pleased to see you, let me assure you."

Jorn muttered something which was doubtless inane —or if it was not he would never know the difference, for he forgot it almost before it was out of his mouth —and sat down. He was not, of course, stunned, for after all, men did hold positions of responsibility here and there; but he was certainly surprised, and somewhat baffled. He was also a little relieved, for an accidental side glance at the stuffy young woman who had been his guide—Ailiss—had captured on her face the identical spasm of disgust which had so upset him in the corridor; but this time it was bent upon the Director. By its intensity now, he saw that it had been meant for the Director even then; it had very little, if anything, to do with Jorn.

Which was very strange, for the man did not seem

to be particularly disgusting. True, he was deformed, which was unusual in this day and age. But he carried it well, and besides, he was hardly a monster; his deformity was not so specific that a name could be given to it. He was only ... somehow out of proportion. Jorn's first impression had been that he was hunchbacked, but actually he was not so twisted as that—at least, not solely in that direction. He did have a hump on his shoulders, but his shoulders themselves were enormously broad, so broad that the hump might have been nothing more, or almost nothing more, than a great knot of muscle which had grown to take advantage of all that leverage. His chest, too, was huge, and so were his arms, particularly his upper arms, which looked capable of supporting aloft the cables of a suspension bridge. Given only this much of him, Jorn could have said no more than that he was obviously a physical giant.

Yet obviously, he was not. Jorn could not see the lower part of his torso, since that was hidden behind the desk, but the head atop that magnificent keg of a chest was disconcertingly small, and supported by a correspondingly scrawny neck. The forearms tapered almost into sticks, at least by contrast to the mighty thews above them, and ended with hands absurdly narrow and delicate.

And most incongruous of all, the Director was old. The stringy neck was wrinkled, the hands were knobby and freckled, the scalp bald and discolored, the face pouchy, the mouth white with the whiteness of creases stretched flat by a full set of dentures. Were you to look first at the eyes, furthermore, you would think by their intricate red stitching of broken capillaries that the Director might be as much as seventy-five years old...

And then you would not; for those bloodshot eyes

were as green as lightning, and as full of danger. Suddenly Jorn realized that the Director had been waiting calmly, all this time, for Jorn to take his measure—and had been watching how Jorn went about it. Jorn tried to look away, embarrassed and confused, and promptly found it almost impossible to do.

The Director smiled frostily, and ended the mutual inspection with a peculiar writhing gesture of his whole visible body, as though he had flexed all of his great anomalous muscles at once. As a warning? Or was it simply some titanic equivalent of a shrug? Jorn found it impossible to tell, especially since the Director was the only person in the room except Dr. Chase-Huebner who was not wearing the odd coverall, which Jorn was now quite certain was a uniform. Instead, he wore a loose-fitting kind of smock, fastened only at the collar and the wrists, which allowed the strange muscular convulsion ample play without revealing enough of its details to permit Jorn to interpret it.

But at the very least, Jorn was abruptly surer than ever that he was out of his depth. Perhaps that was all that the Director had intended. If so, it was thoroughly convincing.

"I suppose you have realized, Mr. Birn," the Director said at last, "that this is essentially a project in space research. I don't of course know at what point in the tests this occurred to you, but at least I observe that you are still with us. So let me ask you this: are you still interested in the job?"

His voice, a light tenor astonishing in so big a man —or was he indeed so big?—at first rather distracted Jorn from the substance of what he was saying; and then, Jorn found the question itself very hard. Finally he said:

"I think so, sir. I wouldn't be interested in any of the ordinary projects in space research that I hear about in the press— I'm, well, not quite ready for suicide. But this one looks like something different; if so, I'm still interested."

The Director smiled a wintry smile. "Exactly so," he said. "Then, I'll proceed. This project emerges from a discovery in basic physics called the Ertak Effect, named after me, as is quite proper since I'm its discoverer; my name is Helminth Ertak. This effect is primarily that of the propagation of patterns—patterns of any kind—to remote, pre-selected areas of space. They go as transforms of the motion-waves of their constituent sub-atomic particles, but essentially without losing their integrity . . . Forgive me, Mr. Birn, but you have the expression of a man who is not following me very well."

"I'm hardly following you at all," Jorn confessed. "The terms are more or less familiar, but I can't seem to make them coherent."

"Then we'll skip the theory—there'll be plenty of time for that later—and concentrate on the consequences. Primarily, what I was looking for was some method of communication with interplanetary ships and planetary colonies which would be reasonably fast, preferably instantaneous if that was possible. One reason we have so much trouble in recruiting for space research is that we can't keep in decent touch with our volunteers once they're launched. They come to feel as though they'd been abandoned very early in the game, which effectively they have though through no fault of ours; and somehow or other, the word leaks back home, and results in just such an attitude toward ordinary space research as you have just exhibited.

Once the glamor wore off it, it became known as a form of suicide—mostly because we couldn't think of any way to talk to the volunteers, once they were in space, without a long time-lag between sentences."

Ailiss cleared her throat ostentatiously. Ertak ignored her.

"However, the Ertak Effect provides us with the means of communication we needed. Though alas it isn't instantaneous, and probably that hope was impossible of realization from the beginning, it is at least *much* faster than the velocity of light. In fact, it's better than twenty times as fast, which is certainly a substantial gain, wouldn't you say?"

"I was taught that beating light speed was impossible in itself," Jorn said faintly.

"So was I. Nothing so irritates me as physics-by-fiat. But that's not all, Mr. Birn. Shortly after we began to develop the necessary apparatus, we discovered that the Ertak Effect provides much more than a fast method of communication over long distances. It can send a physical object just as well as it can send any other sort of pattern. Both, after all, are simply problems in information transfer; they differ only in their orders of complexity. Transforming this implication from theory into hardware took a long, weary while, but we have now done so."

He paused expectantly, but Jorn was again quite lost. He could only shake his head helplessly.

"To be brief, then," the Director said, "we now have a practicable interstellar drive."

"Inter*stellar?*" Jorn whispered slowly. "With . . . with a ship to go with it?"

"The ship is in the building," Ertak said, leaning back in his chair. He was visibly satisfied with the sensation he had produced by his summary, though certainly he must have seen it many times before in other interviews. "And we are surveying suitable target systems. There seems to be no shortage of them, especially since the first trip will be wholly exploratory, with no attempts at planet-falls. We might even skulk around the area of the Great Nova while we're at it, just to get a close look at the remains of an event which influenced our history so much. Why not? It would only add a few months or so to the trip!"

Jorn could find nothing further to say. The Director seemed slightly disappointed.

"Well," he said at last, "this is why you're here. We are building only one ship, necessarily; but we are recruiting two crews, the one to understudy the other. You are only the fourth man to get through our primary screen, so we owe you a choice. Providing that you survive the secondary screening—and the training programs thereafter—which crew would you like to be on: the working crew, or the stand-by?"

"The 'working crew' is the one that will actually go on the trip?"

"Yes," Director Ertak said. "The stand-by crew is only to replace washouts, or men invalided out, or killed in some accident—the great Unforeseeable."

"I want to be in the working crew," Jorn said, without an instant's further hesitation.

For some reason, this did not appear to please Ailiss O'Kung. More surprisingly, it did not appear to please the Director much, either. He turned to the girl with a petulant expression and said crossly:

"You are going to have to do something about your primary screen, Ailiss. It's selecting out nothing but would-be heroes—and we *do* need a stand-by crew, after all."

"I can't control the way you phrase your final questions," Ailiss said between white lips. "If you *will* call the number one crew the 'working' crew, then of course every jobless drone who gets through the primary screen will opt for it. Try calling it the 'throwaway' crew and you'll see the trend reverse completely—as I've already recommended till I'm all out of patience."

"I see you are," Ertak said drily. "But let me remind you that a complete reversal is not what I want either. Each man on the stand-by crew needs to be emotionally ready to go, if we should need him. However, you have a point. I'll take it under advisement."

"That's what you always say," Ailiss said; but the Director abruptly seemed to have given up heeding the bickering. So, in fact, had Jorn Birn, who was suddenly overwhelmed by the realization that he had a job.

And not just any ordinary piece of suicidal space research, a ghost of Jurg Wester reminded him silently. These people didn't do things by halves. They were going to send him to the stars.

"That's enough," Ertak's voice said sharply, cutting through his bemusement. "Mr. Birn, it now becomes necessary for you to go home and settle your affairs; we will send you further instructions in twenty-one days. The rest of you, report to me tomorrow as usual. This session is closed."

And once more, the Director's body was briefly convulsed by that anomalous, pulsing shudder.

3

You mean you really *got* it?" Jurg Wester said, in hurt disbelief. "What are you going to do, anyhow—drop out of the satellite station in a barrel and see how high you bounce?"

Jorn looked critically at his only dress nightgown, stuffed it into his luggage, took it out again and threw it into the trash chute. He was not very much astonished to find how little he owned that was worth anything at all, even to him; but it was surprising to find that most of his few prized possessions were now also quite meaningless.

The vegetable-grading process also helped him to delay answering Jurg, whose question annoyed him in at least six specifiable ways and in an indefinite number of others which he could not at the moment identify. Jorn had never specifically been told not to discuss the job outside of room a-10-prime, but he nevertheless retained a strong impression that he had better be discreet. Ertak and company had not made any attempt to tell their applicants what they were applying for, and if Jorn's experience was typical, the secret never got out except to those who had been accepted. If that was the way the Director was playing it, it ought certainly also to be Jorn's, at least this early in the game.

"It's space research, just like you said it would be," Jorn said. "And it's outright suicidal as far as I can see. In fact it's the craziest thing of its kind I've ever heard of."

"What kind of thing is it?"

"I don't think I'm supposed to say. But Jurg, damn near everything you said about it in advance was right. I don't see any harm in telling you that, since you smelled it long before I did."

"I'm not half as sure of it now as I was then," Jurg said darkly. He watched with obvious incredulity as Jorn jettisoned a threadbare but otherwise perfectly good formal shirt, with his name embroidered on the pocket and a delicate pattern of berries and leaves appliquéd along the sleeves. "If it's all that suicidal, why are you so hot for it? It doesn't make sense."

"Because I'm sick and tired of these barracks, and sick and tired of being useless, that's why," Jorn said. "It's a job, and I've got it. All of a sudden that's enough for me. There's no law that says *you* have to like it. I'm the guy that's taking it, and I like it. Isn't that enough?"

"I suppose so," Jurg said, nibbling gently at one fingernail. "I don't know. I mean, Great Ghost, Jorn, how could I know? What *is* it, anyhow? You can tell me, I won't blab ... but I've got to know. You're a pretty sharp article, I've known that all along, you wouldn't let yourself be trapped into any deal that was *just* like what I thought it was. What's the difference—the kicker? Come on, you've got the job, and I'm still stuck in the conclave, as useless as ever. How did you know to grab for this, while I was still thinking it was hopeless? I need to know; I missed out this time, but I don't want to miss out the next. You've got to tell me."

Jorn straightened slowly and looked at Jurg. He still disliked the man as much as ever, but he could hardly deny that in that burst of candor he found more to admire than he had ever seen in Jurg before. But what more could he tell him?

"I don't know how I got it," Jorn said at last. "They take you through a whole day of tests, and a lot of them are rough. After I passed them—and I don't know how I managed that because most of the time I didn't know what they were testing me for—they told me what it was all about, and asked me whether or not I wanted to go along. I decided that I did, but maybe I was out of my head to do any such thing."

"Do you think I could pass?" Jurg said in a low voice, looking down at his sandals.

"I don't know what to think. I don't know how I passed—so how could I know about you? But, Jurg, it is space research. Is that what you want?"

"I want a job," Jurg said. "You haven't told me much and I suppose you can't. So all I can think is that if you could get it, maybe I could too. Then I suppose I'll make up my own mind whether it's suicide or not. And whether or not I want to commit suicide that badly, in that particular way. Is that how it goes?"

"Yes," Jorn said, closing his valise and shutting the snaps. "That's pretty much how it goes."

"All right, then I'll take a stab at it," Jurg said, standing up. "And if I get it, Birn ... Um."

"Um? What's the matter?"

"Another question. Can I take Koth?"

"Sure you can. You'll have to leave her behind for part of it, but you'll get her back at the end."

"Good. Okay. I'll see you there."

"You've left a speech in midair," Jorn said curiously. "You were saying, if you got the job—"

"Yes, if I get the job, I'll thank you for steering me to it. But don't expect any more pats on the pants, Birn. You made a point of being secretive about it when you left, and what's more there's a lot you could tell me that you haven't, and don't think I don't know it. If I make it all the way, it'll be on my own steam, not because you went out of your way to help me. After that, devil take the hindmost."

"And the hindmost's familiar," Jorn said, shrugging and turning back to his puny suitcase. "That suits me fine."

And in fact, he realized, he had not answered one of Jurg's questions as candidly as he might have, though only because he had misunderstood it. Obviously the substance of the question about Koth had been whether or not she would be allowed along on the trip itself, not just during the interviews and testing; and about this Jorn had no information whatever, only an automatic assumption which might very easily be wrong. After all, presumably mass economy would have to be practiced even more stringently aboard an interstellar vessel than it had to be in local interplanetary spaceflight.

But then, the entire status of the familiars was ambiguous, not only in the area of Director Ertak's project, but in society in general. Wholly a product of the laboratory—the most complex life-form the biochemists had yet managed to produce—they belonged to no group in nature, had no real relatives or taxonomical status, no past nor any role in the drama of evolution. It was generally agreed that they were sexually differentiated; but there were not and had

never been any males of the "species"—they repro-
duced parthenogenetically, and even that only under
highly special, highly artificial conditions. Though
they looked like a sort of animal and were popularly
supposed to be such, even that question had not
entirely been settled: their lack of digestive organs
and their extremely simple nutritional needs were
almost mold-like in character, so that many experts
maintained that they ought to be thought of as sapro-
phytes, rather than true parasites. On the other hand,
their defensive teeth, their mobility and their obvious
—if limited—self-consciousness and awareness of their
environment were not plant-like at all.

Even the popularity of the creatures had come
about through a long series of flukes. Their parasitism
was a necessary condition of their existence; the biochemists had not yet been able to turn out an inde-
pendent entity of that degree of complexity, and many
of them, sensitive to the possibility of a charge of
manufacturing vermin, were not in any hurry to try.
The fact that the first successful experiment had been
performed by a man had made all the succeeding
generations dependent upon traces of testosterone and
other androgens in their "diet"; and this nutritional
prejudice, plus the advantages that the creatures took
up no living space at all, cost nothing to maintain, had
no fleas and required neither bedding nor toilet facilities, had all combined to transform a hapless test-tube
freak into an almost universal pet in the short span
of fifty years.

In that time they had proven their right to be regarded as truly living creatures by their marked in-
dividuality and the unpredictability of their behavior.
In that sense it had to be admitted that fifty years of
experience with them had raised many more questions than it had resolved. The woman-dominated

government viewing with purse-lipped matronly disapproval the obviously compensatory and symbolic aspects of the man/familiar relationship—especially among the vast masses of jobless bachelors—developed powerful urges toward banning them. However, a two-year fact-finding commission was unable to turn up a shred of evidence that the familiars were harmful in any way, except for an unexceptionable tendency to bite anyone who seemed to be menacing either the creature or her master. If nevertheless there was subtle psychological damage being done—the suspicion that had launched the inquiry in the first place—it proved impossible to demonstate.

It did not seem very likely, Jorn thought with regret, that any male allowed into the crew of an interstellar ship would be permitted so purely supernumerary a piece of baggage. The deprivation, it it did take place, was going to seem strange. He had had Tabath since he was thirteen years old—she had been a birthday present from one of his fathers. If his relationship with her—always trouble-free, sometimes amusing, often comforting, and by now almost as automatic as his relationship with the strange person who lived inside his skull—had also been damaging in some hidden respect, there would be no faster way to find out than having her stripped away from him for good and all; for she would not last until his problematical return. She could live only a little over a day without him.

The prospect was anything but pleasant.

He saw the last of the residence conclave on the twenty-first day. From then on he was permanently stationed, not in room a-10-prime, but in a geographically indefinite, quasi-abstract entity simply called The Project. Its headquarters was an immense camp and launching field, ultra-secure behind high wire fences in the middle of an appalling salt desert, located Jorn could not say where. He was flown there, along with four other recruits (all female), and saw only that the government rocket spent most of its time crossing an ocean, by a route which was devoid of any checkpoints he might have been able to recognize. Quite possibly this was unplanned; since Jorn had never before flown in anything that went higher, faster and farther than a jitney before, he knew nothing about how to read terrain from a great altitude.

The camp on the salt flats, however, proved to be little more than a sally-port for Jorn and the other recruits. Though there was obviously a great deal of construction, testing and other activity going on there, Jorn was allowed to take part in almost none of it. In the first six months of his training, he was somewhere else almost all of the time; he knew only that he had travelled at least half a million miles in that period— at least, because he had spent three weeks of it on the Moon.

He was equally sure, on less evidence, that he must have travelled at least that far again going round and around in giant centrifuges; in riding rocket sleds down horizon-to-horizon lines of railroad track; and most mysteriously, in sitting patiently or doing exercises in isolation chambers firmly fixed to the earth, while his weight varied steadily and smoothly from nothing at all to close to nine times normal. He also covered considerable ground crawling flat on his belly dragging a carbine behind him, as though interstellar travel were going to be a sort of infantry operation; conversely, he learned to read terrain from the air in innumerable glider drops over every imaginable kind of landscape.

During none of this—gruelling, outré and bodeful though most of it was—did he hear any suggestion that he be deprived of Tabath; and in time the possibility, though it was actually still as great as ever, receded from the forefront of his attention and went underground. If the familiar herself found the training alarming, she gave no sign; or, more accurately, she seemed to find the world she lived in almost continuously alarming, precisely as usual, but dismissible as long as she could continue to ride through it on Jorn's arm.

Of all the rigors he was forced to undergo, one of the most difficult to bear up under was the fact that his section leader was Ailiss O'Kung. Obviously she had been through it all before, perhaps several times, and regarded the gasps and struggles of the recruits with easy contempt; though she allowed no one to fail through unfamiliarity or exhaustion, her definition of these two categories only barely distinguished them from stupidity and gold-bricking, with both of which she was utterly merciless. And yet, oddly, she lost fewer recruits than any other section leader.

Though he tried to tell himself that the impression was nonsense, Jorn was nevertheless convinced that Ailiss went out of her way to assign him the roughest, the dirtiest or the dullest details of every assignment. Since it was impossible to discover a reason for this, he was forced to invent one, this being the instantaneous dislike she seemed to have taken to him when they had first met in room a-10-prime.

In response, he swore in private, gritted his teeth and bore down harder. Simple male pride was not going to allow him to admit that a girl was any better at all this than he was (the simple fact that she *was* better notwithstanding; she might be better at it now, but he'd show her). Somehow it quite failed to occur to him that approximately the same thought might be being cherished in the heads of every male in the section, and that Ailiss' attitude was expressly designed to provoke nothing else. As for the women in the section, they were mostly a hardy, uncomplaining, almost offensively cheerful lot, who quickly became frighteningly competent, and seemed to have no threshold of boredom whatever.

At the end of the six-month period, the section was broken up and reassigned, in groups of two and three, to new and more specialized types of training. This still left Jorn and Ailiss stuck firmly together, since he had been so unfortunate as to show talent in piloting and navigation, which was her own area of specialization.

In the new section, for the first time, he found himself also yoked to Jurg Wester.

The encounter took place, wholly inconveniently, during Jorn's second flight to the Moon—much different from the first one, in that now he was turning a trial trick as cadet astrogator. Working under Ailiss, he allowed himself to become rattled at the computers during turnover and was sent down to the ward room in disgrace . . . and there was Jurg, looking passing smug.

"Well, Great Ghost," Jurg said. "It's the boy wonder, himself. I thought they were going to feed you to the meteor-eels, long ago. Don't tell me you're in my section!"

"It looks that way," Jorn said. He looked Wester over carefully. He was wearing a brassard which marked him as a temporary lance-corporal, only a recruit rank but nevertheless higher than Jorn's own. This had the makings of a bad situation. "Is this your first lunar trick?"

"It sure is. Old Corporal Wester was in no hurry.

All the same, it seems I'm a stripe or so up on you already."

"So you are. Congratulations."

"It wasn't luck, I can tell you that." He grasped Jorn by the elbow and lowered his voice confidentially, although there was no one else in the ward room. "Listen, maybe I shot off my mouth a little the last time I saw you, but you know I didn't mean anything by it, don't you? Old Big Mouth Wester, I just love to sound off. But I owe you a favor for putting me on to this nice soft berth. And seeing as how you haven't got a stripe yet, maybe I could give you a tip or two. Let bygones be bygones. Okay?"

"Fine," Jorn said. "Only I don't see what's so soft about it. You had to go through most or all of what I did or you wouldn't be here, let alone with the stripe. And it didn't strike me as so soft."

"Oh, I *work*," Jurg said scornfully. "I work like hell and I make a big impression—when I have to. I was the only man in my old section who never goofed in plain sight. I always do everything exactly by the books, even if it's nit-witted to do it that way. That's what The Project says it wants and that's exactly what I give 'em, right down the line."

"All right, but if that adds up to a soft berth, I'll still take concrete," Jorn said, baffled.

"You're not using your head, Birn, I can see that. For instance: who was your section clerk?"

"One of the women—you wouldn't know her. She was top-notch at it, too."

"No doubt," Jurg said. "But in my section, I was clerk. I saw to it that I was. You'd be surprised how much a simple thing like that can save you in wear-and-tear on the feet—and in hours of sleep."

"I sure would. In our section the clerk's job was an extra; it didn't save the girl from even one of the

regular details. She did it nights, for a proficienty rat-
ing, and if the strain had slowed her up in the field,
she'd not only have been broken but gigged to boot."

"Your section boss must be crazy," Jurg said.

Much as Jorn had learned to loathe Ailiss O'Kung,
he knew this proposition to be untrue. Ailiss did not
differ sharply from the few other section leaders he
had had a chance to observe, except that—unhappily
for Jorn—she was better than they were. Suddenly,
he thought he had the answer.

"Jurg," he said, "are you stand-by or throwaway?"

"Stand-by, naturally. I'm not going to let a job like
this be a one-shot proposition. You guys can have the
heroics—"

And then his eyes narrowed. "Oh, ho," he said.
"Maybe I've been cutting my throat all this time, eh?
I suppose this is your *second* round on the Moon?"

"Yes, it is."

"So you're a brevet officer?"

"No, not now. I was cadet navigator, but I just
finished lousing it, just before I came down here. For
all I know I may have had it for good—or at least have
to start again from the bottom."

"Somehow I doubt it," Jurg said, his voice turning
ugly very gradually. "All this time I've been trying
to give you a hand, you've been standing there with
that klax-eating grin on your face, congratulating
yourself that crewmen rank stand-bys regardless of
stripes. Big-hearted Wester! Well, enjoy it while you
can, Birn, because I'll tell you something I don't think
you know—since you let a woman interpret the rules
for you; Throwaways don't rank stand-bys *until they're
actually on the crew*. It doesn't go for recruits like you
and me."

"I never thought it did," Jorn said stiffly.

"I'll bet you didn't. But just in case you did—when

we get back from the Moon, I'm going to demonstrate the principle. Then we'll see how long that smirk of yours lasts."

"I sort of doubt," Jorn said, remembering the month after his own first lunar assignment, "that you'll find the time. But you're welcome to try."

"Birn!" Ailiss O'Kung's voice came stingingly through the ward room annunciator. "On the bridge—on the double!"

Jorn took off without bothering to make any manners. His last glimpse of Jurg Wester's face was not reassuring.

Turnover had already been completed by the time he swam his way back into the control cabin, but the atmosphere there was anything but the usual one of cautious relaxation preceding a low-gravity landing. On the monitoring screen from back home was the face of Pol Kamblin, The Project's senior astronomer, whom Jorn had come to know slightly since astrogation had come to be his own principal cross. He was at a loss to account for such high level supervision of Ailiss, who was more than competent to handle much trickier landings than this; yet Kamblin's face looked frighteningly stern.

"Computers," Ailiss said briefly, without looking away from the ranked data board before her. "I want a conversion to a cislunar ellipse with an intersect at Salt Flats—as close as possible to one hundred per cent on momentum. And we'd better have landing fuel left, or I swear I'll have your hide in the Hereafter."

"But there isn't enough—"

"There's got to be," Kamblin said quietly from the screen. "You've got forty-eight seconds to pick your orbit. Better move."

Jorn moved, without wasting another second in wondering if this might possibly be another test—with the lives of everyone aboard dependent on his skill. The dilemma at bottom was simple: computers are hundreds of times faster at calculation than human brains are, but they are also idiots; they have to be programmed by a human brain, or they will say nothing about any problem but, "Duuh?"

He worked faster than he had ever dreamed he could—even as recently as half an hour ago. When the answer came through he had no idea whether it was right or wrong, nor was there any time left in which to find out. He fed the figures to Ailiss; the rockets fired briefly; and then the ship was beginning its long slanting fall around behind the Moon.

The mountains slid beneath them like thousands of saw-toothed fangs. Only after the ship crossed the terminator, and the moonscape was plunged into darkness, did Jorn think to recheck his figures. They seemed to be right.

They had to be. There was not a drop of reaction mass available for corrections.

"I check you," Ailiss said suddenly. "That's the way it's *always* supposed to go, Mister—flat out with all speed and correct the first time."

Jorn said nothing, which was what was expected of him. He was reassured, a little, but the margin was still going to be too narrow for comfort.

"I check you also," said Kamblin's voice. "Provided you don't run into a storm on the way down. I'll call meteorology and report back." The screen went blank.

"Damn," Ailiss said. "I was going to ask him why they loused up my mission."

"He didn't give any hint at all?" Jorn said, emboldened by this sudden outburst of confidence.

"Not much. The Director has called a joint meeting of staff and crew, for right now, or maybe ten minutes sooner."

"And you've no idea why he might do that?"

"The only reason that occurs to me," Ailiss said grimly, "is that the funds have been cut off—and The Project is cancelled. Stand by, here comes Kamblin with the weather."

Even the Director's big office could not have contained a joint meeting of staff and crew, if by "crew" was meant all trainees, both stand-by and throwaway; Ertak had to settle for the brevet ranks alone. Nor could he have his meeting "right now or ten minutes sooner," for a number of the people he needed had been long distances away at the time the call went out —some of them farther than Ailiss.

Nevertheless, when the meeting assembled, twenty-five rumor-filled hours after Ailiss' and Jorn's last-tea-cup-of-propellant landing, it was sizable enough. Most of the people there Jorn had never seen before, or seen only briefly without knowing who they were. Besides Ertak and his four personal staffers, there were Ailiss, Dr. Chase-Huebner, Kamblin, and all the surviving members of Jorn's class and their section leaders. (This, however, did not include Jurg Wester; there were no stand-by trainees of any rank present.) The staff members who would command the stand-by crew were, however, there in force. Of them, Jorn recognized only Toni Cook, the stand-by captain. The red room was decidedly crowded.

"Thank you for your promptness—in some cases the cause of considerable personal danger to yourselves," Ertak said, in his light wintry voice. "I would not have asked you to take the risks had we not been confronted with a crisis of the very first order—in fact, of a unique order. I am not very well equipped to explain that and I am going to give the job to Dr. Kamblin in a moment. First, however, there's one other thing on my mind."

He swung his head toward Ailiss.

"Lieutenant O'Kung, we are going to have to discard your new nomenclature for the crews. It turns out that in the four months we have been using it, we have done ourselves considerable damage."

"In what way?" Ailiss said coldly.

"It has seriously deteriorated the quality of the men we've been recruiting as stand-bys. While I was waiting for you all to get here, I had some samples taken among the stand-bys available to me here at the base. The sampling shows that fully a third of the stand-by recruits we now have think of the training, hard though it is, as essentially a make-work kind of labor camp. If those men were suddenly asked to go on the actual mission, they'd panic."

"I don't think so," Ailiss said. "I pre-tested their attitudes in that area, naturally, Director."

"Did you throw them the proposition itself, as an immediate reality?"

"No," Ailiss said. "There were a good many obvious reasons why it wasn't advisable."

"Maybe it wasn't then. It's advisable now. *I* threw them the question—and they break like paperboard spoons."

Ailiss was silent for what seemed like many minutes, though in actuality she made a quick recovery. "Then, granted that the nomenclature should be changed— and that we'll have to jettison those men. But what moved you to such an extreme test in the first place, Director?"

Again that peculiar writhing shrug, which seemed to involve the Director's whole upper torso. If it still aroused the same revulsion in Ailiss, her expression this time did not betray it.

"The fact," Ertak said grimly, "that we *are* going to need to use both crews—at a minimum. Time we got down to business. Dr. Kamblin, please take the floor."

"Certainly," Kamblin said. He stood, quite unruffled. He was really quite a big man compared to Ertak, but he was older, and there did not seem to be much drive to him. Despite his eminence in his field, many decades of subjection to women had made him non-committal about anything that mattered to him, a man determined only to avoid becoming involved. "The situation, as briefly as possible, is this:

"As you're all too well aware, the solar pulsation cycles have been getting increasingly out of phase in the last century or so, and the solar constant has risen by as much as a thousandth of a percentage point. Thus far, these things haven't much more than inconvenienced us. For example, they've given us hotter summers than we like; and they've made weather control increasingly complex, sometimes even unmanageable.

"Nevertheless, we—the astrophysicists and other scientists, I mean—were interested in finding out the *why* of the changes. At first it was very difficult to unearth any clues. The Sun seemed much the same as ever, consisting mostly of hydrogen, with circulating traces of magnesium, oxygen, aluminum, silicon, phosphorous, sulfur, chlorine, argon and potassium—all, of course, in highly ionized states, and in traces only, since most of these elements are at the core of the star, invisible to our spectroscopes. (Forgive me the catalogue; I assure you it's necessary for proper understanding of what follows.)

"Nor did the solar constant at first provide us with any clues. The very slight increase corresponded to no infra-stellar process that we could account for. As for the other findings, I'll summarize by saying that they were all quite consistent with a star of our Sun's age and mass.

"It was only when we applied the increase in the solar constant to the *core* of the Sun that we found what was happening.

"In brief, the heart of our Sun has now become sufficiently dense so that the temperature there has passed 2,000 million degrees, in a hell of stripped and mangled nuclei and intense gamma radiation such as no finite mind could hope to imagine. At this temperature, the familiar metallic trace elements are beginning to undergo fushion. We have already picked up the first faint shadow of a titanium line. Soon we shall be seeing vanadium; and after that, with increasing rapidity, chromium, manganese, iron, cobalt, nickel and zinc. The rest of this history, alas, we know all too well.

"We have seen it before."

This time the silence was actually long, and screaming with shock and tension. Jorn had no need to ask any questions. Though he had not understood a tithe of the technicalities of Kamblin's explanation, the astronomer's final remark could have reference to nothing else but the Great Nova.

The Sun was going to go, the same way.

After a while, Kamblin went on, almost in a whisper. "We were fortunate in several ways, as a planet. For one, consider the great distance of our orbit from the Sun; since you've been studying other nearby systems lately, you'll have some appreciation of how unusually long our One Astronomical Unit is. Secondly, life apparently evolved here very late, after our Sun had gone through most of its swelling phase—a process which takes about a thousand million years for a star the size of ours. But it is just as bad, I'm afraid, to arrive at the end of this process as it would have been to have suffered its growing pains."

"How much longer will it last?" one of the section chiefs asked.

"Not very long. The core temperature will have to reach 5,000 million degrees before the explosion takes place, and that may take a good fifty years—"

"Fifty years!" Ailiss said raggedly. "Dr. Kamblin, that's not—"

"I know," Kamblin said gently. "It seems a stunningly short term for an astronomical process; but bear in mind, Ailiss, that all such processes are exponential, and that this one has been going on for a thousand million years already. By now it is proceeding very rapidly, more so every minute.

"And I am very much afraid that in actuality we have much *less* time even than that. I won't afflict you with the thermodynamic and geometrical arguments involved, but simply remind you that the solar constant, too, is going to continue to rise. By the time it has risen just five per cent, this plant will be uninhabitable. It will still be here for a while, but there'll be no life on it."

"How long?" Ailiss repeated.

"Nine years," Kamblin said. "It will be possible to work during the first five of those, perhaps during the sixth. Then we will begin dying . . . and at the end of the ninth year, everything will be dead . . . even the bacteria."

"Work? What do you mean, work?" Jorn said almost angrily, finding his voice at last. "Work at what? Obviously there's nothing we can do. This is the end, for all of us."

"The end only for most of us," a musical male voice

said from the back of the room. Everyone turned except Kamblin, Ertak and his staff, who of course were facing in that direction already; none of them seemed to be in the least surprised by the interruption. From the rest of the gathering, however, there arose a gasp of stunned confusion.

Even for those barely possible few who did not recognize the man himself, the ceremonial blue and gold robes told the tale: he was the World Consort. His presence could only mean that whatever he had to say was the contribution of the Matriarch herself.

"I an here essentially to answer the young man's question," he said. "There *is* work that we can do—work for a whole people, for a whole world. One Ertak-drive ship is no longer enough; we want hundreds—even thousands if that is possible. We are transforming The Project into a mass crash program for the survival of the race. We are going to build, man and launch a fleet."

Nobody spoke. There was no comment anyone could have made which would not have been ridiculously inadequate to the grandeur of the goal.

At long last Ertak cleared his throat and looked around the red room as if seeking waverers. He found none.

"All right, Lieutenant Ailiss O'Kung," he said, "start weeding."

It was necessary, of course, but it would have been far better for everyone, now and later, if the necessity had not arisen at all. That apparently had been Ailiss O'Kung's fault—but she had made her recommendation in good faith, and had to be allowed one mistake; if you shot everyone for the first such, you would never have a next generation. Besides, the mistake was Ertak's as well—after all, he had allowed himself to be persuaded, and had turned the recommendation into practice.

Jurg Wester was weeded.

He sought Jorn out at the anteroom of the armorer's shop, where Jorn was worriedly awaiting a prognosis on his spacesuit's homing compass, on Jurg's last day at the base. Jorn would far rather have avoided the confrontation, both for obvious reasons and because his training had so intensified that he had no spare minutes worth mentioning. But in a way he too was responsible for Jung's having enlisted in the first place, so he listened patiently.

"I just want you to know," Jurg said in an even voice, "that this outfit dosen't fool me for a minute, no matter how well they manage to bamboozle you. Do you think I don't know what the news is, already? I saw to it that I had a friend at the meeting, you can take that from me. I know about the nova, and I know about the fleet."

"All right, why not?" Jorn said. "There's always a grapevine, especially on a thing this size. I don't see what harm it does. Everyone in the world will know in another week, anyhow."

"They'll know what they'll be told, which will be half lies," Jurg said. "Ertak won't mention that he busted out most of his best men to begin with, will he? *He* knows that he'd never be able to call those boys incompetent and make it stick—not on me, and not on most of the others he's booting into the beltways. But it won't do any good for them to clam up about it, because I know the story already, and I'll see to it that it spreads."

"What story?" Jorn said, confused. "Why do you care what I think, anyhow?"

"Because I think you might still be salvageable, once you get the superiority klax pounded out of your head.

They fired me and the rest of the boys out of The Project because they're going to pack their survival fleet with women. What else? It was another matter when a star-trip looked like pure, expensive, 'disinterested' research. Then, men were plenty good enough to throw away on it—the usual suicide fodder. But now it's different, isn't it—now that only the people on those ships are likely to live more than five or six years!"

"That makes no sense," Jorn said. "They won't perpetuate the race very well if they concentrate on one sex."

"Oh, they'll carry a few studs along—nice complaisant types." Jurg did not specify whom he meant, but he hardly had to. "At least that's obviously what they're planning. Well, I may upset their pushcart for them before they're done. I didn't go along with their Project for a ride to the stars, in the first place."

"I remember your telling me you didn't. But Great Ghost, Jurg, if you didn't want to go, they why are you making such a fuss about it now?"

"Because *now* I·want to go, hero. And I'm going to go. I haven't made up my mind whether or not to take you along. Think about that a while. The boys and I have a lot of very valuable military training under our jackets right now, thanks to The Project— and The Project is turning us loose with it. It'll be no trouble to pass most of that training on, to as many cadres as we have men for noncoms. We even have a few little items of equipment we're taking with us— and it won't do you any good to blab to old wormy Ertak about that, because we've got them taken down and distributed among us in a way none of his female inspectors and other trained animals could detect in a million years. We had a long head start on this *before* The Project, by the way. Then it was a men's liberation movement. And it still is.

"By the time you start loading your ships, the government that built them won't be in existence. The next one will be a government of *men*. Men, not studs. Think it over, Birn. There's still time for you—but not much."

He turned, shouldered his pack, and took one step away. Jorn made a two-miscrosecond confession of complete wrong-headedness to his own soul, and sent Jurg the rest of the way out the door with a whole-hearted, near-paralyzing full field kick.

It was 100% the wrong thing to do, and it was deeply satisfying.

What Jurg's response might have been, after he recovered enough to realize what had happened, was a question never solved. The two guards outside picked him up, dusted him off, and led him toward the gate with a gentleness which was in fact only an optical illusion. Soon he was out of sight.

There was a *tsk* of disapproval behind Jorn. It was the armorer, a motherly doe sergeant of about fifty whose heart was wrung by the slightest malfunctioning of any device, particularly if the device was supposed to be lethal. She was carrying Jorn's homing compass, in an advanced state of disassembly.

"Some of those stand-bys had such big feet," she said. "It's just as well not to have them stumbling around inside a starship. They might break something . . . As for this compass, it's gone. I'll issue you a new one. It's a shame there isn't time to slip it into your friend's pack, along with the other tinkertoys."

Jorn grinned his relief. "Then you heard what he said."

"I hear everything that goes on in my own shop,"

she said. "Once I step out the door, I'm deaf as a post."

"Well . . . don't you think something ought to be done? I mean, like alerting the inspectors, so their packs can be pulled apart as they go out the door?"

"They don't have anything worth stealing, my dear," the sergeant said. "My goodness, you don't think I'd let anybody leave my base carrying anything dangerous, do you? After all, they might *hurt* somebody. Just sign here, and here, and I'll issue you your compass, that's a good boy."

Jorn signed and the sergeant disappeared back into her shop. He felt considerably better.

All the same, it was perfectly true that the survival ships' passengers—as well as their crews—were going to be women, by a vast majority. After all, that was only a matter of simple biology: one man could start an almost unlimited number of children; but one woman, only a few at a time.

Nevertheless, it rankled.

4

Being young, Jorn was not immediately able to rid himself of his notion—no, it was more than a notion, it was a fact of his brief experience—that five years was a long, long time in the future. He was astonished to see how rapidly Ertak and his staff forced themselves to make huge decisions, which ordinarily should have been weighed for several months at the very least. Now four or five of these might be made on a single typical day.

For a sufficient example, take ship design. The Project's ship on the ways, the *Javelin,* had been planned as a vessel which would return home well within the lifetime of its original crew. Now it had to be thought of, instead, as a colony-in-flight, able to shelter many generations if necessary. It was of course perfectly true that there were three other solar systems near enough to home to have been detected by the satellite observatories; also true that this implied, with a statistical trustworthiness vanishingly close to unity, that planets were a part of the normal life history of any star; and that these facts logically implied the existence of thousands of home-like, hospitable planets within the *Javelin's* theoretical range.

"But all three of those systems are effectively binaries," Kamblin explained in one of his regular orientation lectures to the crew. "That is, the 'planet' we have discovered going around each of those three stars is a gas supergiant so huge that it's almost hot enough to shine by its own light . . . what we call a 'gray ghost,' to big to be a planet and yet not quite large enough to be a dwarf star either. It's very unlikely that either of the two primaries in such a system will have habitable planets—though of course one ship or another will be able to pass close enough to each system to check that. No, gentlemen, we are all going to have to sweep a considerable volume of space . . . and be much attended by luck."

But spaceships which will also be colonies are not easily designed from nothing; and an intersellar ship which was specifically designed *not* to be a colony cannot speedily be torn down and changed over. When presented with the time-budget for such an operation, Ertak decided almost instantly against it. The *Javelin* was ordered to be modified in as many small ways as possible, but she was not to be rebuilt, nor was she to be nibbled at drastically enough to risk weakening her present structure. This made sense, but Jorn was not prepared for the corollary decision: that all the *Javelin's* sister ships were to be built to the same design and with only such minor modifications as the *Javelin* herself could safely withstand. This decision too was eminently reasonable, but not to a man to whom five years seemed like a long time.

And as with the ships, so with the world. This decision was not Ertak's to make, but since the principles were the same, so was the outcome. The whole world was *not* converted overnight, or at any other time, to the production of intersellar ships, as Jorn had fuzzily imagined the World Consort to have implied. Doom or no doom, the fact remained that the original *Javelin* at completion would have cost half a billion credits, plus four years in construction time. Her sister ships would cost slightly less than that, but not much—mass production is an almost meaningless term for a structure like a bridge or a skyscraper or a ship, the savings involved running narrowly between two and four per cent per structure.

Jorn had of course supposed that mere financial cost—and in that word "mere" there resounded hollowly a huge hole in his education—would go by the board in so ultimate an emergency. Like all the poor, money to him was an abstraction, a frivolity, a curse; as a graduate engineer he knew all about oil, but nobody had bothered to tell him money is even more necessary and valuable. Skyscrapers, battleships, satellite stations or survival fleets all require a high-energy economy, which means that almost all the goods and services in the world—and hence almost all of the money—must continue to be devoted to keeping that economy at the highest possible level. The farmer may not leap from her combine and take up a hammer on the nearest incomplete intersellar ship; the submarine freighter engineer may not abandon the engines which are propelling titanium ore or sponge platinum from one continent to another; the baker may not cease to make bread; the banker may not take her hands away from the guidance of credit, the raw material of political unity and the only enduring testimonial to man's confidence in man; even the newscaster may not cease from telling all the rest, who in fact do not know how to hold a hammer and cannot feel or see the escape fleet growing, that grow it does, and any job well done is an investment in The Project.

All this takes money; nothing else will serve.

"Of course we're trading for the moment on the fact that most of the people don't really believe a word of it," Ertak remarked. "They're willing to go along because the government's buttered on a little inflation; that's how you ease civilians into any war. But that won't last long enough. By the end of the next year the bombs will start falling, and then they'll want to run the war themselves, for their own personal protection. That's when the trouble begins."

"I don't see the analogy," Jorn confessed.

"I mean that by that time they'll be beginning to feel the heat—all of them, not just the neurotics who think they can feel it now. It'll occur to them that the Sun really *is* going to explode. Then they'll begin to wonder what they're really working for: in other words, whether or not what they're doing is going to get them an entrance ticket to one of our ships. And the moment we have to start paying them in hope instead of in credits, we'll be in trouble—and there won't be a ship in the fleet that's much beyond half done at that point, except of course the *Javelin*."

"But we are going to be carrying pasengers," Jorn said hesitantly. "Lots of them."

"My dear Jorn! Never mind, Ailiss O'Kung says you may be a great navigator . . . Of course we'll be carrying passengers—roughly a hundred for every crewman on the *Javelin*, and even more on the others. But how many people does that come to? We won't know until we see how many ships we manage to build before we have to leave, but I'll tell you this: under the best possible circumstances, the total population of the fleet will be less than the differential birthrate of this planet *for one single day*. Probably a good deal less."

"Still, Director, we won't be taking the old, or the handicapped or . . . certainly not the newborn . . ."

"Ah," Ertak said with a frozen smile. "That makes it look much easier. But let's do a little simple multiplication, by tens. The *Javelin* will be able to carry about twenty-five hundred people. If the fleet consists of a hundred such ships—which would astonish me—then it will leave carrying a quarter of a million. Correct?"

Jorn began to feel sick. The Director saw it, obviously, but he continued his explanation without mercy.

"Now let's suppose that you've managed to disqualify twenty-five *million* people, on sure sound principles. This leaves you with 2,475,000,000 eligible candidates from which to pick 250,000. About one from every ten million. Would you like the job?"

"No," Jorn said. "Great Ghost, no."

"I don't blame you," Ertak said. "In fact nobody wants it. But all the same, my dear Jorn, somebody is going to have to take it."

Ertak did not take it, nor did anyone else who was known to Jorn, even marginally. Perhaps the Matriarch herself did; if so, it was never written against her name. Nor against anyone else's.

The slashing, ruthless style of it might once have been Ertak's signature, but this time all such decade-ponderable decisions were being made in his style, overnight, on every level. And possibly only the Matriarch could have killed off so much of the world on principle, long before the moral agonies of even so ruthless a man as Ertak could have been much past conception.

Item: No marginal farmers.

Item: No piece-workers.

Item: No administrators—whtther private, government or technical; that was what the crew was for.

Item: No drones.

Item: No infertiles; no disabled; no one over 30, except on the crews; no one under 17; no one with a family history of cancer, insanity, epilepsy, mycobacterial infection, opposition to the Matriarchy, or about two hundred other genetic or possibly genetic defects; no one with a personal history of (nearly five thousand) medical conditions; no one convicted of a major crime.

Item: No one who had left a job without cause within three years before the launching. (The "without cause" clause was window-dressing; the government had no intention of making any check on causes, let alone entertaining any appeals.)

Item: No parasitic skills, such as brokerage or advertising.

Item: No doctors, no engineers, no mathematicians, no astronomers, no unique skills in the sciences or in engineering not already included in the crews.

. . . And much more. It was a chillingly inclusive list. Some of its categories included the equivalents of whole nations. Very little of it was ever made public; there were some parts of it which were never even written down; and some others so coldly slaughterous that they could not even be deduced by anyone not charged with the choices involved.

But it served, for a while. It cut the choices back, especially during the privileged period when the world did not know that they were being cut back. At term, there were left only a single million possible choices for each passenger.

And in the end, it became impossible to disguise

this piece of elementary arithmetic, or to protect the migration from it, even with the greatest ill-will in the world.

"And besides," Dr. Chase-Huebner said gently, "I am afraid that in all conscience we must also leave the animals behind."

Ertak leaned forward, splaying his elbows out on his immense desk. In this position his shoulders loomed so large that it was hard to imagine how his torso could support them; but his voice was oddly subdued, even defensive.

"It's a little late for vegetarianism, isn't it?" he said. "Or being kind to animals? We've ruled people out by so many millions, we can hardly start trying to trade cows for them."

"Of course not," Dr. Chase-Huebner agreed. "I wasn't talking about meat animals. We need them; vegetable proteins are incomplete. We'll have to carry cattle and carry them alive, for breeding. No; what I'm talking about are worms, and the like."

Ertak's shoulders heaved slowly. "Go ahead," he said. "But make it brief, please."

"I can be as brief as you like," the biologist told him, compassionately. "You knew it would come to this I'm sure. And you know that I don't mean to mount a personal attack on you, Hari; give me that much credit."

Ertak said, "It isn't a question of credit, mother." The obscenity escaped into the air without either of them seeming to notice it. "You were always a scientist, and so now am I, or something like one. We face each other as accomplished facts. Simply tell me what you mean; that's sufficient." He shuddered again. "I'm not unequipped to argue the point—but do me the favor of recognizing that I already know what it is."

"I'm not so sure Hari. You've been too busy with your drive fields and your proving-stand tests and your training programs to think about worms, or bacteria, or all the other insidious parasites—tumor cells included—that you assigned to me. I've been thinking about all these things, as you asked me to do. Now I'm ready to report:

"The familiars *will* have to be left behind."

"Justify," the Director said. "Pound for pound—"

"—is a nonsense way of approaching the question. Those are not the parameters that we need to fill. Better an ounce of canned fish than a pound of familiar—they're mostly water, and they're inedible, useless, even unable to adapt: dead weight."

"A woman would naturally say so."

"Perhaps. But as I say, that isn't even the argument."

"No? Then what is?"

"Contamination," the woman said quietly.

"Now you're talking nonsense. Familiars contaminate nothing."

"Nothing here, at home. But who knows what will contaminate a virgin world? Do you know how huge a role epidemics have played in the history of mankind? The books tell us the name of the man who discovered a given continent, but they don't tell us the name of the man in his crew who picked up that continent's epidemic disease and brought it back home with him—back to whole populations that had no immunity to it at all. And who among us is going to take the responsibility of infecting a whole new planet with the mycobacterium, the spirochete, the plague virus, the white death—*or the familiar,* that unknown, unclassifiable thing we have made ourselves? We can't swear as yet that the creature is harmless even to us!

"You don't answer. Well, then, I shall have to answer for you. I say: Nobody. I am empowered to rule on such questions—and I so rule."

After a while, he inclined his head, once. This seemed to be victory enough, for now, considering how well she knew what it had cost him. She smiled gently and made as if to take his hand; but he did not look up and she thought better of it. With a formal murmur of thanks, she turned and left the group.

Finally, the Director's chest and shoulders stirred again, and the movement flowed down his right sleeve, puffing it out above his forearm, which was resting on the desk. From the cuff there snouted out a flat, narrow head, as pink and freckled as Ertak's own hand, and almost as big. It stared at the closed door by which the woman had left.

Then the still air of the red room was split with a scrannel hiss, like the sudden escape of live steam.

Jorn had no time to puzzle over the sudden inaccessibility of the Director; everything abruptly was going too fast. The five years had in fact almost gone by; and the fleet was, both by definition and a long accumulation of miracles, well more than half done. By now, Jorn was better equipped to understand the awful logic of the simple theory of numbers involved, which ruled that a fleet half finished today may tomorrow have to be dubbed, arbitrarily, all the fleet that there is going to be.

"And we are very close to term now," Dr. Chase-Huebner told a meeting in the red room. These days she spoke for the Director; if anybody knew why, nobody had been able to tell Jorn. "We have thirty ships. A thirty-first, the *Haggard,* is far enough along to be counted in."

"What about the *Assegai?*" someone asked.

"Out of the question. It would take more than a year just talking about the heat and the storms, either—though both are awful enough already. Public panic is rising so rapidly now that we won't be able to keep workers on the *Assegai* another year without promising them all a berth on her; and as you all know, our complement is filled. Believe me, I hate to leave that ship behind—I hate to leave any ship behind, but particularly the *Assegai* with her refinements. But we have to stop somewhere. It would be nice to wait for the *Boomerang,* too; on paper she's far and away the trimmest ship of her class on the ways—but at the moment she's nothing but a keel and a heap of loose I-beams. This has got to be the end."

"Why not call a halt on the *Haggard,* too?" Kamblin proposed. 'She'll take another five months, it seems."

"Because," Dr. Chase-Huebner said gently, "we have a crew and passengers for the *Haggard,* and the Director dosen't mean to leave anyone behind whom we have promised can go."

From what little Jorn knew of Ertak, this did not seem very like the Director; but perhaps the doctor herself had somehow persuaded him to so rule. But then, suddenly a thought so wild that sheer surprise prevented him from censoring it came tumbling out of him in a rush.

"If so, how much government are we carrying?" he heard himself demanding, in a voice at the same time cracking with alarm as he overheard his own temerity. "The Matriarch, I suppose; and how many others?"

Dr. Chase-Huebner stared at him. Her expression seemed to be one of reproachful astonishment; but

all the same, for the very first time since he had
known her, he found himself afraid of her.

"Nobody else," she said, in a silken-soft voice. "Nobody at all, not even the Matriarch. We have chosen
and trained everyone honestly, and we are not taking
anyone just because she happens to be Somebody."

That should have been that; and for a few seconds,
as Jorn subsided into an agony of embarrassment and
self-recrimination, it was. But then Ailiss O'Kung said
precisely:

"Does that include the Director, Dr. Chase-Huebner?"

"Naturally," the physician said, without even blinking. "We could hardly do without him, after all."

"I raise that question, if you please," Ailiss said
grimly. "I understand he has suffered a breakdown.
Other people have been weeded for less. Do you still
regard him as competent?"

"I do. That closes the question, I trust?"

"Not quite. Will you allow me to test him?"

The two women were now rigidly face to face in
a furious locking of gazes whose import was totally
beyond Jorn's understanding.

"For what purpose?"

"To confirm your assessment. Competence among
crew members is my responsibility."

"You have often been wrong," Dr. Chase-Huebner
said.

"Sometimes, often, never, I won't argue. Nevertheless, I am the psychologist *responsible*; you are not."

"Very well," Dr. Chase-Huebner said with a gentle
smile, folding her plump, magnificently competent fingers together. "In that case, you are discharged. Let
us proceed."

"At your peril, Doctor," Ailiss said, as though she
were driving nails. Jorn had never seen her looking

so downright ugly before; her mouth was white, her cheekbones stood out like flying buttresses, even her eyebrows seemed to have become blacker. "I think I know why you're now speaking for the Director, and why he has *not* suffered any breakdown. And why you have not extended the ruling you tried to make to include all the other ... to include the rest of the crew. You're afraid of universal breakdown of ... those elements ... if you do promulgate that ruling; so you are going to take the Director along instead."

"I don't find such vague talk worthy of comment."

"You don't find it in the least vague, Hary't. Do you think that the Matriarch will stay home and die for her people once she knows the facts? In the face of ... in the face of such wholesale ballasting of—"

"*Stop*," Dr. Chase-Huebner said, her face working. After a moment, she managed to become a little more composed. "All right, Ailiss, you may be right. I agree that you should talk to the Director; on some points, obviously, you won't be convinced you're wrong until he tells you so. But in the meantime, this discussion is explosive in the extreme; it had better be closed."

Insofar as Jorn could read Ailiss' expression, she was about to agree to this baffling, inconclusive proposal; but she never had the chance. In mid-air in Ertak's office a siren groaned briefly, urgently, and on Ertak's desk, just to the left and directly in front of Dr. Chase-Huebner, the orange light went on.

It had never been on before. It would never go on again. It meant, very simply, that Dr. Chase-Huebner —and Director Ertak?—had already waited too long, and that even the *Haggard* would now never be finished.

The Sun, baleful though it had become, was still decades away from its last agony; but the cataclysm was upon them, all the same.

5

The truck was covered and there was hardly anything to be seen from it. Jorn and fourteen other crew members of the *Javelin* clung to the hard benches and craned their necks around each other, trying to peer out the back over the tailgate; but at first the administration building blocked off the view, and then the driver was careening across Salt Flats at a pace which made visibility less important than just hanging on. It was maddening.

All the same, a general distant roar of human and machine sound, massive and ugly, came rolling clearly over the snarling of the truck's own engine. If the sputtering of gas guns was a part of that clamor, it could not be distinguished, at this distance, from the boundary fences; but there were louder explosions too —explosive bullets, grenades, even an occasional mortar.

It was hard to believe that any sort of a mob could have gathered outside that fence, in the middle of one of the most forbidding deserts in this entire hemisphere of the world; but that was what the orange light had been triggered to foretell. And the fact that the mob was already here—and that the truck was already racing for the *Javelin*—could mean only that it was huge, armed, and at least partially organized.

And it also meant, Jorn was fervently sure regardless of the evidence, that somebody—a great many somebodies—had badly misjudged Jurg Wester, and the likes of him.

The flickering night framed over the tailgate of the truck was streaked briefly by the track of a rocket shell. The concussion from the tank-killer hung fire long after the wake of the little missile had vanished, and its residual image after it; and then, *blam*, there it came, from somewhere in the middle distance. Obviously it hadn't been aimed at the truck, which in any event was showing no lights; but it left behind no doubt that the mob was armed. Of course at this speed a tire blowout would kill Jorn and everyone else almost as instantly—

The tires screamed and the truck, yawing and lurching, slammed down to a dead stop, piling all fifteen of them up against the back wall of the cab. Accompanying the yell of brakes and tires was the awful grinding, pounding note of gears being stripped: the driver had shifted down into first in order to stop shorter than the brakes could manage alone, trusting to the crew's field gear to protect them and her own skill to protect her.

They were still trying to unscramble themselves from their own swearing black homologous knot when the tailgate clanged down. "Out!" a woman's voice shouted. "Hit that lift! Lock closes in seven minutes! *Move!*"

Jorn recognized the voice. It belonged to the armorer. Well, that explained the drastic driving. She was waiting for them as they unscrambled and struck turf, carrying a hooded torch further hooded by her gauntlet, between two fingers of which she allowed only a razor-edge of red light to shear at the ground. Even in the dim monochrome, however, Jorn could see that she was bleeding a black rill from one nostril.

For an instant thereafter he was totally confused. Then, against the starlight, he picked out the colossal shaft of the *Javelin*, sweeping motionlessly into the sky as though she would never end. Beside her, seemingly clinging to one long dully-gleaming curve, was the delicate scaffolding of the elevator, waiting to be extinguished like a flame at the moment of take-off.

"That way," the armorer growled, "*that* way." She gestured along the sand and salt with the razor-edge of the torch; but Jorn was already running. He could hear others behind him. Far away, something—a bomb?—burst open with a deep, heavy groan, and a minute temblor shook the desert under his pounding feet.

Then the aluminum deck of the lift car was ringing with the trampling of boots as they charged aboard, shoving each other and grabbing for cables or struts they could only guess were there. "... thirteen ... fourteen ... Now by the Ghost ... All right, get *in*, dammit, *fifteen!*" A whistle warbled shrilly, almost in Jorn's ear. The cab shuddered, and then, without any pause, lurched skyward with a muscle-wrenching jolt.

After that, it did not seem to be going anywhere at all, despite the piercing, unpredictable screams it sometimes uttered against its guide-rails, and the jittering of the deck beneath their feet. Nevertheless it was rising, and as it rose, Jorn could see more and more of the outskirts of the base. Now they were seething with light and smoke, all along the perimeter. Tracers criss-crossed the hot night air in all directions. The higher the car inched, the more likely it seemed to Jorn that everyone on it would be riddled before they would be able to reach the faraway airlock of the *Javelin.*

Then, ages later, they were high enough to begin to see the general shape of the attack. It was huge. Beyond the immediate, writhing lines of fire along the fences, twinkling processions of vehicles were racing in nearly straight lines over the desert toward Salt Flats. Near the horizon there did indeed seem to be some bombs falling, and some of these small "nominal" atomics. Evidently the government still controlled the air—which was good as far as it went, but the planes would be under strict orders to stay well away from the ships, where the main part of the mob obviously was concentrating, and hence the only place where a really comprehensive explosion might be decisive.

The lift quivered and rose a little faster. It brought them all high enough to test their handholds with a heavy buffeting of wind—though the wind seemed to be just as hot as the air on the desert itself had been. There would be no more cool winds on this planet, not at any altitude at which a man could expect to breathe, not even on the mountains.

Another rocket shell went searing past in a high hazy arc. Jorn stopped breathing for an instant. That one *was* close. Didn't they realize that they might hit the ship itself? For that matter, didn't they know that they couldn't pack all of those thousands of people into the *Javelin* and her sisters? Didn't they know that they'd wreck her, just trying? Sure, there were three other ships standing on Salt Flats, but—

But as he realized the futility of trying to think like a mob, his mind repeated, *"thousands* of people," and quailed. That mob was being held off only by the stand-bys and there were very few of those any more,

certainly far from a full extra crew for each ship.
They had been weeded; and judging by the rocket
shells, many of the rejects were now howling on the
other side of the fence. Despite the stand-by training,
and the supernal lethality of their gear, the stand they
were making was suicidal. They would *have* to fall
back, or—

But they did not fall back. Not this time.

They were broken open.

About two miles northwest of the administration
building, the line of flame sagged inward. Then it
went dark along at least half a mile; the fence was
down. Outside, there was a flaming surge of movement toward the hole like surf foaming around a
whirlpool.

The cab came to a bouncing stop in the middle of
the sky.

"All right, inside!" the armorer shouted. "Lock
closes in one minute! Inside—shuffle or dust!"

Had that whole crawling ascent been only six minutes long? But there was no time for post-mortems.
The sixteen of them were packed into the lock like
fish in a jar, and the outer door swung ponderously,
unfeelingly shut on the battle and on the whole outside world . . . for good.

As it sealed, a hairline semi-circle of light, intolerably brilliant after the near-blackness of the field,
began to widen on the other side of the lock. Jorn
was momentarily startled; it had not occurred to him
that the interior of the ship might be fully lit—
although, since she had no ports, there was no reason
why she shouldn't have been; and besides, her passengers had been living aboard her ever since she was
finished. In the first influx of light he was startled to
find Ailiss O'Kung standing next to him, white and
sweating with strain.

"Very good," the armorer said, a little more quietly, but not much. "Posts, ladies and gentlemen. And thank you."

Proper enough, Jorn thought deliriously, since the armorer was the only one in the party who was not an officer. Still the speech had all the irrationality of a dream.

Everything had been rehearsed over and over long before this. Jorn headed for the control barrel almost by instinct, Ailiss trotting by his side. In the big blinking cavern he ran a fast tally of his navigation section and found them there; he did not stop to count Ailiss' crew, but he had a vague feeling that she was at least one officer short.

Ertak was there, hunched in the command chair above them. That was his right, since the *Javelin* was the flagship. But it was the first time that Jorn had seen him in five years; it increased the dream-like feeling.

The Director did not turn around. He did not even seem to hear what was going on behind him. After a moment, however, he spoke into a chest microphone, and all the desk screens came to life, including Jorn's own. Once again he had a view of the scene outside.

It no longer really looked like a battle, but more like a carnival, confusing, gay with light, without real meaning. Nevertheless, from this height Jorn was able to see that a miracle had happened around the breach at the fence. Somehow, whoever had been generalling the defense had managed to pinch off the inflow, clean up the stragglers, and order a retreat. The irregular closed curve of fire, curiously amoeboid, was well inside the fences everywhere, and drawing closer and closer to the ships; but it was still unbroken.

Beside Jorn's right hand he heard a razzy muttering,

and reached guiltily for his operations helmet. Inside it, Ertak's voice was saying:

"... and maintain routine identification signal census in a continuous cycle. Field officers, continue to hold ground by the *Haggard* and the *Assegai*; they both look finished and we want the rabble to assume that they are. On Signal Red, flatten out toward the *Assegai*; on Signal Blue, let them have her. Lifts are down on *Javelin* and *Quarrel*; repeat, lifts down on *Javelin* and *Quarrel* ... Congratulations, Deep Station. To all hands: Deep Station reports it has secured all five ships.... Census? Census, report! ... Field officers, Signal Red, this is Signal Red, execute ... To all hands: Deep Station is launching ... Census? ... Field officers, supersede previous orders. On blue signal, yield both *Assegai* and *Boomerang* and fall back toward *Javelin*. Fall back toward *Javelin*, we will be last off ... Attention *Quarrel*, cycle airlock and begin countdown; we won't need you for personnel."

The line of fire bulged inward toward the *Javelin*, and then toward the incomplete ships. Then there was an even deeper bulge toward the *Quarrel*.

"Field officers, blue signal will be on count of zero. At the signal, yield the field and board the *Javelin's* lift. One minute allowed for boarding, repeat one minute. Counting toward blue signal: five ... four ... three ... two ... one ... zero, Signal Blue! Signal Blue!"

The line swept inward on all sides—and then suddenly it disappeared utterly. There was no longer even a part of it to be seen. Instead there were only the torches and vehicle lights of the mob, pouring inward toward the three ships they thought they had gained. In a barely perceptible flickering of small-arms fire, what little there was left of the stand-by crew funnelled toward the lift shaft of the *Javelin*, trying to disengage.

"Census, I have pips for twenty-one survivors and a load estimate of eighteen on the lift. Confirm, please.... All right, nineteen now. Time's up. Lift crew, haul them.... Absolutely not. *Quarrel* will leave in six minutes exactly. If we wait for three stragglers, all twenty-one will die. Haul!"

A minute went by. The mob continued to concentrate around the bases of the "captured" ships, like phosphorescent ants, until each of them seemed to be standing in a spreading pool of light. The pool around the *Boomerang*, however, quickly began to seep away toward the others; close up it was self-evident that that ship was radically incomplete.

"To all hands: Deep Station has launched all five ships. We have garbled reports from other stations indicating at least eighteen more either secured or already launched. There are also still two stations holding radio silence; we are hoping this means that their locations remain unknown and they are undergoing no attack."

Three minutes.

"Passenger census ... Well, that's what they get for sightseeing; we warned them. Certainly it could be a lot worse.... Airlock crew, prepare to admit standbys."

Nobody could call them stand-bys after tonight.

Four minutes. There was turmoil now in the pools of light around the *Assegai* and the *Haggard*. Little sparks of light were clambering slowly up the scaffolding of their lift-shafts; obviously they had discovered that the lifts themselves were inoperable.

Five minutes. The airlock was open now, gaping for the nineteen seared heroes. The mob was beginning to ooze tentatively toward the *Quarrel*.

"... seventeen, eighteen, nineteen. Cycle airlock. Field officers, welcome aboard. Get that thing closed, *you've got four seconds—*"

Thoommmm!

The *Quarrel* vanished. On Salt Flats the pools of light were still visible, but they looked dimmer, and completely frozen: truck lights left on, torches fallen from hands.... The concussion had probably killed many of them. The rest would be likely to be still unconscious when the *Javelin* left.

"A clean take-off," Ertak's voice said calmly. "Ship's officers, begin countdown. We will follow in eight minutes." He paused and seemed to check some board hidden by his chest. Then he added, "To all hands: congratulations. The *Javelin* is the last ship able to leave, and the last of these still on the ground. Twenty-nine others are all already on their way."

Thirty ships, Jorn thought numbly. Thirty ships.

"Correction, we are thirty-one in all. We have a signal from the *Kestrel*. She is damaged but off safely."

There was a ragged cheer in the earphones. Jorn did not join in it. What difference could one ship make? What difference would ten have made?

"Census ... thank you. To all hands: we now have a final population check. We are carrying seventy-five thousand people, give or take about a hundred. We have escaped—and by that token, we know that we will survive. Take-off in thirty seconds."

We have escaped ... we will survive. And yet ... how many died when the *Quarrel* vanished, and the lights were stilled on Salt Flats? How many more would die to the departure of the *Javelin*? How many had been killed to keep them out of the ships, all over the world?

We will survive. But who are we to survive?

6

Doubtless some such question was on many minds, but the first month of flight afforded nobody any time for brooding, least of all Jorn. Like all the officers, he was standing two watches out of three, and hit his bunk so exhausted that he frequently went to sleep while still in the midst of removing his clothes.

The chores involved in part emerged from the *Javelin*'s role as flagship of the fleet, hence responsible for its overall direction. The time would come when the expanding cloud of ships would be too tenuous to keep such an arrangement practicable; but in the meantime, the fleet could not be permitted to hurtle off in thirty-one random directions, toward obviously unfruitful or even overlapping targets. Most of the burden of reducing this chaos—a natural outcome of the sudden take-off—to some desirable order, or rather, to a set of such orders, fell upon Kamblin and Jorn; selecting the final order and imposing it was of course Ertak's function and duty.

For the most part, however, the burdens were simply a part of the shaking-down process; every ship in the fleet was having virtually the same experience. Boarding and take-off had been disorderly at best, entirely contrary to plan at worst. Some ships were seriously understaffed; some almost bulging with last-minute refugees. Only the ten ships whose ground locations had remained unknown had exactly the complement of passengers, stand-bys and crew that the plans had called for. A number of the ships were damaged, some only slightly, some seriously.

In particular, the ship's day did not begin without the question as to whether or not the *Kestrel* was still on course. Almost a third of her was useless, and into the remaining two thirds was packed an appalling press of humanity—for she had been the only ship of the five at her base to get away at all. Ertak had twice counselled her captain to turn back, each time to be refused. Jorn could hardly blame the man; between the probability of death in space, and the absolute certainty of being pulled to pieces very slowly after returning home, the choice was narrow but clear. Evidently Ertak thought so too; at least, the Director did not take the risk of turning his recommendation into a direct order.

Finally—and about this there was precisely nothing that could be done—there was the ineluctable fact that the ships had not been designed to do what they were now being asked to do. Coping with their deficiencies as arks was an obviously impossible task, and yet one which had to be faced every day, day after day, end without world. The *Javelin*, since she was the prototype of them all, was the worst ship in the fleet in this respect; but even the most recent, the *Peregrine*, could boast of very few ameliorations of the problem. Jorn hated to think of what daily life aboard the *Kestrel* must be like; luckily, perhaps, he had no time to.

Yet even in the midst of all this feverish, desperate activity there was a common emotion, brooding over everything, difficult to label yet so palpable that Jorn could almost imagine himself breathing it in with the air. People's faces had no expression, as though they had withdrawn almost wholly into themselves. Conversation between crew members was limited almost entirely to duty matters and technicalities, even at mess.

The work load slackened significantly after the first week of the second month, but there was no visible change in mood to go with it. If anything, the silence became even more intense. In part, Jorn was sure, each man and woman was thinking of the tragedy at Salt Flats, and the single enormous fact that all those had died so that these should live. They were the elect; and Jorn at least could not rid himself of the feeling that many of them, surely including himself, owed their election to chance ... or worse. Though he had never understood the meaning of the Ertak affair, the very presence of the Director constantly hinted at some still-uncauterized corruption; and if corruption were there, where else might it not be found?

And elected for what? No one could say. The *Javelin* was outward bound for an unknown destination, on a journey of unknown length in both time and space: a frail steel bubble which might be washed up on any shore ... or burst tracelessly, so far into the wastes that not even a fragment would ever reach any beach, without even the dim solace of a sea-bottom grave to sink to, but only nothing, nothing at all ... For this they had given up everything that had given their lives continuity and meaning up to now; and even where, as with Jorn, those lives had seemed unrewarding to the point of meaninglessness already, there was something about being uprooted forever

that made even the stoniest of soils worth mourning.
There was a song, a very old one:

When I was a pup, I lived in a hut,
My father was a drunkard, my mother was a slut,
    And oh, my love, how the rains came down;

We had not to eat, neither bread nor meat,
Not a rag for our sores, nor shoes for our feet,
    And oh, my love, how the rains came down;

Take a fortune for your fee, it's no matter to me,
For last week I journeyed that hovel for to see,
    And oh, my love, how the rains came down;

It was burnt to the ground; not a cinder to be found;
And I fell upon my knees, as I had a mortal wound,
    And oh, my love, how the rains came down!

He had, he realized, never understood it before.

And yet behind them their sun still burned, only a
point of light now but still the only star in their sky
with a magnitude greater than —2. As the months
went by and they gradually forgot the insane storms
and the blasting heat of their last year at home, it
seemed less and less credible that so immemorial a
friend and companion might explode. Everyone knew
that the explosion was supposed to be decades in the
future; some few of them even knew that there was
doubt as to whether or not the ships could be far
enough away from it to be safe, even after all that
time in which to flee at even greater velocities. Yet
there the Sun shone still, as always, unchanged except
to the photographic plates and diffraction gratings of
Kamblin and his assistants, who kept their own
counsel.

The reaction was inevitable. Within another two months, the unrelieved gloom of the shakedown period was gradually transforming itself into its opposite. It took the form of an almost childish interest and delight in the total novelty of the new life, both in its abstract, scarcely visualizable goals and in its intimate details. Some of the passengers, and many of the officers and crew, even became interested enough to feel disappointed that the *Javelin* would not, after all, pass anywhere near the grave of the old nova, which had played so crucial a role in history. (The ship was, in fact, going almost directly away from that unquietly dead star. Ertak was following a Great Circle in the galactic plane, counter to the direction of rotation of the lens as a whole, hoping to take at least a little advantage of the contrary motion to increase the number of systems the *Javelin* might encounter. Since the ship had shared that rotation on take-off, it would be a long time before any such gain could begin to show.)

Steadily the new mood grew stronger. If leaving home had been death, then perhaps this was rebirth, with all its hopes of avoiding past mistakes.

Those on the bridge also had the diversion of the Grand Log. It had been agreed long ago that every ship should keep a common fleet log, as well as a log of its own; so that when some ships were destroyed or lost—which everyone knew to be inevitable, though it would not happen to *their* ship—the unique records might not be lost with them. This entailed a great deal of inter-ship chatter—much more, in fact, than was strictly necessary: everyone involved realized that this kind of fraternization was not going to be possible for more than a few years, even with the Ertak communicator. The globe of ships was growing too fast.

Almost nobody listened to any messages from home, though those, since they came in by radio, would be cut off much more quickly—as soon as the *Javelin* passed the speed of light, as she would by the end of her first year in space. But the new mood was too fragile to test with the corrosions of whatever was being broadcast at home, even with that large majority of messages which were not intended for the fleet at all.

Kamblin, however, listened; he had to. Eventually, he was forced to ask Ertak to call together the officers for a report.

"I won't burden you with any specifics about content, since I'm pretty sure you don't want them," he said. "But the changes in the Sun are going rather faster than I had anticipated, and I couldn't account for them by any solar process; so I had to have recourse to the radio to see if they were real, or just an artifact of the time-velocity relationship."

"And are they?" Ertak said, startled. "I certainly would have predicted that they wouldn't be."

"But they are, Director. It's lop-sided and I think I can show you why; there is no accompanying mass effect, and having found that out from theory in advance, you must have assumed that the contraction equation was meaningless under the conditions of your drive-field. I made that assumption too, but with the evidence now in hand, I can see where the error lies."

"What does it mean for us?" Ailiss asked.

"Right now, all it means is that the radio broadcasts from home are beginning to sound a little tinny, despite the fact that they should sound *lower* in pitch the faster we go away from the source," Kamblin said. "But it will mean a good deal more than that to us later. I'm still uncertain of the exact figures, but it looks as though the accumulated error will be about thirty per cent."

Ertak nodded, but Ailiss said promptly, "Sorry, I'm not reading you. Error in what? Which parameters are you filling?"

"Real time and acceleration," Kamblin said patiently. "Here, look at it this way. I set the date of the explosion at about forty-five years after take-off. That's when it will happen, back home. But for us, time is gradually speeding up. For us, the explosion will happen about thirty-one years after take-off."

"Oh. Well, that still seems to be a fair distance in the future. And we'll be just as far away from it as we thought we'd be, if it's only a relativistic effect."

"It isn't only a relativistic effect," Jorn said suddenly. "It's either that or it's *entirely* meaningless!"

"Easy, Ailiss, that isn't what he means," Kamblin said gently. "I don't think he's talking about physics now. What is it, Jorn?"

"Well ... It's going to be bad for us. It means that the people home are going to seem to have less time, too, from our point of view. I can't do contraction equations in my head or I could tell you how much less."

"Don't try, I know already," Kamblin said. "The effect is small on this end of the curve, this early. For us, it will seem that our planet will die after we have been about three years in space—instead of the predicted four. And we've been out nearly half a year already."

"And you've been *listening* to them?" Jorn whispered. "It must be an inferno back there."

"It is wholly horrible," Kamblin said gravely, "and it will get much worse. That's why I bring the matter up now. It could have waited, otherwise. But in view of this, it seems to me that the general cheerfulness on board ship lately is not only unwarranted—it's extremely dangerous."

"It is," Ertak rumbled. "It is. But there's one thing about it that's absolutely certain: It won't last.

"Give them a little time to reflect and the hopefulness will give way to despair and then—well, mark my words, the cheerfulness won't last."

7

And of course it did not. As the year stretched out toward its end, bringing closer the moment when nothing more could be heard from home thereafter, more and more people began to vote in the wardrooms to hear whatever was coming from there. Kamblin had suggested that access to those broadcasts be confined to the bridge, but the Director overruled this, for reasons he did not see fit to explain.

The messages all came through originally in a high, disquieting chittering which had to be recorded and played back at well under its reception speed to be intelligible at all. Even then, not very much that anyone could comprehend came through. Entertainment broadcasting had long since died, that was clear; now nothing was being transmitted but routing orders, pleas for help, hard news in hard codes, and other matters of official business whose purport could not be riddled. The tropics were gone, scorched to the ground, and the temperate zones were afire in many places. Those who remained alive huddled at the poles, dying of heat prostration and starvation in about equal numbers, under skies permanently black with smoke.

Incredibly, there was a war on between the two poles. Nobody could guess what they had found to fight about. They no longer seemed to know themselves.

And yet, and yet, in some unguessable crypt of this blistered, blackened, burning world, there was a sane man—

The signal was quite strong compared to the others, and directional. Furthermore, it was slowed by just the necessary amount, so that it first came through as a strange groaning noise, and had to be picked up direct instead of on the tape. It said:

"Calling the Interstellar Expeditionary Project. Don't try to reply, I'll never hear you. If my figures are right, you're about to cross over the speed of light. May the Ghost bear you in His hands. If you find any worlds, make a better job of them than we did with this one. Can't say any more but will set this to repeat—"

Then there was a heavy explosion, powerful even at this enormous distance; and a woman's voice, screaming:

"Thought you'd get away clean, did you? Thought we couldn't find your little spy's den, eh? Somebody kill me that traitor!"

A crackle and hiss of shots; a groan; the laughter of several people, sex not determinable; retreating footsteps, somehow unsteady. And then, another groan, and the slow, slow onset of terminal breathing.

He took a long time to die. Then the recording began again:

"Calling the Interstellar Expeditionary Project. Don't try to reply, I'll never hear you ..."

Somebody, surely, should have turned it off. Many left the ward-room at their second hearing of the woman's voice; many more after the man died a second time. But there was still a little knot of listeners around the public-address speaker when, eight repetitions later, the *Javelin* crossed smoothly over the light barrier and the broadcast slid downward sickeningly into eternal silence.

And with this, Jorn realized in a gray mist of horror, their flight had actually begun.

If Ertak had thought that the reaction might include some form of violence, he did not get it. The shock was too great for that. The response was more than just the old depression come back full force; for not only did the broadcast bring home to the *Javelin*'s people the full horror of what was happening back home, but it was known to be the last message the *Javelin* could receive from there ... until the Ultimate Message of the explosion itself. Thus with the gloom there came back guilt, tearing at the liver like a bird of prey.

Not that anyone could sensibly believe himself responsible for the heat and the smoke and the war and the insanity. Nevertheless, the fact that those on the *Javelin* were no longer there to share these things brought with it a sense of responsibility which reason could not shake off. It was the feeling of having gotten away with something, and hence accompanied, as always before, by the conviction that punishment could not be deferred forever—and probably was imminent.

This time, however, though it was much more intense, it did not last so long; the distractions, their way smoothed by habit, took command more rapidly. Neither the depression nor the guilt vanished entirely, but it became possible more and more to ignore them. Time was going about healing over the wound; there would of course be scars, but it was no longer acutely painful, diminishing first to a chronic twinge, then gradually into an ache, and from there into an unsensed emotional disability which was its last and lasting residue.

In this they were helped by the *Javelin*'s steady acceleration, which had already brought her well past twice the speed of light. It was no longer possible even to see the Sun, except with complex instrumental systems depending upon the Ertak Effect which were available only in the control barrel. These consumed significant budgets of power, easy to provide from the fusion generators but not at all easy to handle, and Ertak saw no reason—nor did anyone else on the crew —to make such special glances backward a part of the general transcasts to the ward-rooms. Mostly, nobody needed them but Kamblin. They were not missed.

And again, coping with the exigencies of shipboard life was bound sooner or later to take precedence over any abstract emotion, no matter how powerful; it was immediate and minute-by-minute, the commonplace and tragic treachery of daily living to grand sorrows and grand loves alike.

There were, for example, many more women among both passengers and crew than had originally been planned. They had been packed on board, in the plans as well as in fact, at what had been effectively the last minute—that is to say, when the Interstellar Expeditionary Project had been converted into a survival armada—for the same reason that the IEP had first planned to include women only among the officers: because they were regarded as too rare and valuable to risk suicide. Originally, it had been very clear, the IEP was to have been like the usual interplanetary probe in this respect: something that one threw away drones on. Jurg Wester (and where was he now? a carbonized mark among many on the floor of the furnace that had been Salt Flats?) had been right about that, as about some other things.

Because of this change in plans and procedures, the women on board the *Javelin* had far less privacy than did the men, despite every attempt at rearranging the ship, simply because there were fewer facilities of all kinds available for them. This drawback was in addition to the fact that there was very little privacy available for either sex, or for both as a unit. There were few corridors anywhere in the ship; they had been torn out. Cabins, where they existed at all, simply gave on other cabins, so that in proceeding from one task to another one was constantly forced to happen upon and bull through the most personal kinds of scenes. This was so commonplace that even the habit of apologizing for it was dying out, and the habit of seeking privacy, though much more stubborn, was dying away in its wake. There was a theory current aboard ship that this kind of physical openness—and it was not merely erotic, but included everything from scratching to plumbing—was good; but it was equally easy to find partisans of the opposite view. One aspect of it, however, was undeniable: it was fatal to sexual possessiveness and jealousy. The customs of some five centuries back, when love-making had been regarded as often a team sport and almost always a spectator sport, were undergoing an obvious renaissance on board the *Javeline* (though the fact was not read into the Grand Log, nor was it reported from any other ship in the fleet; as usual, the letter was showing itself far more durable than the facts).

It was also gradually becoming evident, as the calendars ticked inexorably on, that it was true that males are more adept with machinery than females are, despite the vast number of women in the past society who had made successes in engineering and other mechanical trades. Even in the fabric of that society that assumption had been built firmly, for it had been standard, as Jorn himself exemplified, to give a surplus male an engineering education. The theory was that if such a male were ever needed in a hurry, he would be most likely to be needed for that sort of task—or, at the least, that that was the best one could do toward training him to be proteanly useful. This had seemed to be a workable arrangement in the relatively static matriarchy—though its long-run practicality would now never be known, for the matriarchy had been the first society of its kind in the history of the world, and it had been young when it died—but that whole balance was now completely upset. Aboard the *Javelin* the males were rising ineluctably into the ascendancy. They were, first, suddenly in short supply to service the mechanical details of ship life—and almost all the important details of ship life were mechanical in the broadest sense of the word, ranging from apprentice ship's electrician to Ertak's ability to handle complex mathematical abstractions as though they had some bearing upon real life. ("A female mathematician is historically as unlikely an object as a female composer," Kamblin had once observed—privately—to Jorn. "There've been a few of each—but never a good one.")

This was no longer a theory, but a fact of the situation in which they all had to live, and upon which all their lives depended. Nevertheless many of the women aboard the *Javelin* found themselves unable to adapt to it. Time after time, in large matters as well as in small, they were betrayed into revealing that they still thought of themselves as part of a power elite, definable simply by gender. It was often annoying, sometimes infuriating, and once or twice had been actively dangerous; yet in retrospect Jorn found that he could not remain indignant for long. It was hardly their fault. After all, they had been born and raised in a society where they *had* been a power elite, as he had been born and raised in one where he had been something not much better than trash. That kind of deep, irrational conviction is notably difficult to unlearn, and in fact is never unlearned entirely.

Nevertheless shipboard society, as a new society in itself, was showing increasing signs of strain from this source. The passengers were the first to feel it, since they had relatively less to do with their time (though they were by no means idle—no one could be). The first sign was a sudden surge of covert and then open promiscuity, followed by an equally sudden outbreak of family realignments, the latter usually signalled in advance by midnight scuffling and snarling and morning black eyes. At this stage the strain was not so noticeable on the bridge and in the control barrel, but it was there, and growing.

It grew steadily as time went by, daylessly, nightlessly, but without let or surcease. In the five years—could that be right? Yes, incredibly, it had been that long—since the light barrier had been broken, not a ship in the armada had made an even slightly promising planet-fall. There had been false alarms, but even those were growing rarer, as the ships' computers learned by experience. The keeping of the Grand Log became a duty, and then, finally, a positive chore; there simply was no longer anything interesting to report, except for scraps of astrophysical data which held meaning only for Kamblin and his counterparts elsewhere in the fleet. Otherwise, what each ship found to say was very much like what all the others found to say. The entries became steadily shorter, the attendance at the transceiver more and more perfunctory; often, now, what was written down in the Log was not the full text of the message, and sometimes the message was not entered at all.

"Birn, just what are you doing now?" Ailiss' voice snapped down from the RF bridge. "Trying to figure out what thirty per cent of three is, again?"

"I was thinking," Jorn said slowly.

"Well, do it on sack time. I need those fleet angular momentum corrections *now*."

"They've been on your clipboard for the last twenty minutes."

"Um. Oh. High time. Well, find something else to do. Something *productive*."

Jorn suppressed a retort and bent to faking a job. She had caught him during one of those brief periods —once rare, but they were becoming commoner now —when he was ahead of schedule; but he was not going to let the matter turn into another session of snapping and snarling over nothing if he could help it. He had had more than enough of those already.

Ailiss O'Kung was in fact tolerating the strains of the new society rather more poorly, on the whole, than Jorn would have expected. Jorn found the reaction thoroughly unpleasant. Perhaps the only compensation to be derived from it from his point of view —and it was mainly a gain only for his curiosity, though it did slightly increase his respect for Ailiss at a time when he had lost almost all other traces of it— was that through these quarrels he managed to learn something about her background. She had never let a scrap of that kind of information slip out during the training period, and thereafter there simply hadn't been time, until now. What prompted her suddenly to volunteer what she had so long withheld was unknown to Jorn, but it was his guess—and a good one, he suspected on very little evidence—that she felt forced by her situation into using it to hold her emotional "altitude," not only over Jorn, but in the whole hierarchy of the shipboard peck-order.

And she had been indeed highly placed back home: a scientific attaché to a member of the Matriarch's cabinet, and the youngest person of either sex ever to hold the post. She had surrendered it on her own initiative to join The Project, which had had no such high place to offer her, though to be sure it had placed her as high as it could.

This was admirable, doubtless. But it was no longer of any moment: an empty title in a discarded history, without bearing on the world of the *Javelin*. That Ailiss referred to it at all now meant only that she had failed to reconcile herself to the deprivation of power, and the reversal of status, which she herself had engineered. In this, though perhaps she was an extreme case (or perhaps not), she was far from alone on board the ship; the affliction was as general among the women as a low-grade contagion, and it was ever present.

Their third major enemy, as Jorn was coming more and more to appreciate, was time itself. The median age on board the *Javelin* was slightly over forty. This meant that there were a few babes-in-arms (though more were arriving all the time) and a very few elderly people of both sexes, but that most of the population clustered around middle-age or younger—so closely, in fact, that the average age was a good six years under the median. Life expectancy had stabilized back home, many decades before the present debacle had even been suspected, at around a century for males and between 115 and 120 years for females; and though the hazards of interstellar travel, both known and unknown, could be expected to cut those figures somewhat, there was a general awareness that this kind of communal, cooped-up, low-reward living, with all its sensory deprivations, disorientations, boredoms, frustrations, offenses to the aesthetic sense, and inescapable personal frictions might go on for many decades to come. Indeed, in view of the lack of success of the entire armada thus far, it might constitute all that was left of life, perhaps for generations to come, perhaps—who could tell?—forever.

But they had had the firmest of reminders that even this was better than death: the fate of the *Kestrel.*

It had been assumed throughout the rest of the armada that that problem had settled itself. It had not; it remained exactly what it had been before; but the urgency had gone out of it. The packed masses aboard the *Kestrel* had come to the only terms possible with the intolerable kind of life their damaged ship forced them to lead. The *Kestrel* was still with the expanding sphere of ships, a sort of stabilized slum without hope of relief or rehabilitation ... except by a planet-fall which the *Kestrel* would probably be unable to handle.

Then, in a period of hardly more than three weeks, the inhabited part of the *Kestrel* was gutted from end to end by pestilence.

Maddeningly, the disease was wholly familiar. It was nothing more than one of the twenty-odd known forms of the white death. Yet none of the measures that the *Kestrel* could take, nor any recommended by Dr. Chase-Huebner or any other physician in the fleet, seemed even to slow it down by more than a day. Familiar though it was, the micro-organism responsible had evidently undergone a drastic mutation in the only part of its metabolism that counted: it was totally resistant to anti-bacterial drugs. And since the *Kestrel* was now twenty-five light years away from her nearest neighbor in the fleet, there was no help that could be offered her except useless advice. The end was inevitable.

Suddenly the Grand Log was an interesting document again.

There was some survivors—nothing in biology ever happens 100 per cent, not even death—who had every hope, according to Dr. Chase-Huebner, of being immune henceforth. But from the *Kestrel*'s preceding situation, where she had had far more people aboard than she could keep alive—as the pestilence had belatedly but conclusively proven—the ship had been cut back to so small a complement that they could not even help each other in their convalescences, let alone operate the *Kestrel* herself. In addition, the survivors were unselected. Surveying their losses, and particularly their losses in terms of skills, the survivors set about shutting down most of the rest of the ship. This was for personal survival only, and for the sake of a few possible children in the future, for the *Kestrel* could never make a planet-fall now. Grimly, the survivors set about making her instead into a planet.

But they failed. The food went first. They still had a fusion engineer, who promised them that she could make them anything they needed out of the hydrogen sweepings of the interstellar gas. But by this she meant chemical elements, which can indeed be made by simple, straightforward atomic processes if only enough energy is available; and the *Kestrel* still had the energy. Putting together chemical compounds like protein molecules, however, is of an altogether higher order of complexity, and there was no one left aboard the *Kestrel* who knew how to program the computers who had handled this task before. An attempt to do it by the handbook poisoned half the pitiful remainder, including the only man capable of servicing the ship's one remaining electrical converter; the fusion engineer had always thought simple electricity beneath her notice. The temperature began to drop; the air gradually became foul; and starvation followed after in the cold black caves. The fusion engineer locked herself in with her little sun, and spent her time synthesizing torrents of undrinkable water. Sometimes she could be heard singing.

The prospect of having to listen to this process going to completion, and entering it duly in the Grand Log, was almost too much for anyone in the control barrel of the *Javelin* to bear, though it had its fans in the ward-rooms; but they were spared this. Among those aboard the *Kestrel* whom the plague had passed over, there was evidently still one brave woman ... or man.

The *Kestrel* ceased to exist. No one saw it go, but suddenly it was gone, beacon, carrier wave and all.

Exactly what happened could never be known, but all the same there was hardly any doubt about it. Someone had had the ultimate courage to blow up the ship.

"But could so few people do it?" Jorn asked, afterward.

"One person could do it," Ertak said somberly. "That's the penalty that complexity pays. It takes thousands of people to keep an enterprise like the *Javelin* alive; but only one man can kill it ... if he knows how."

Jorn shuddered. "I wonder ..."

"Um. What?"

"I, I was wondering if I'd have had the nerve. The Ghost award him, whoever he was."

"Yes," Ertak said abstractedly, shifting his shoulders as though they were a burden to him. "Or whoever she was. But there's more to it than that, Birn. Do you realize what a hole this leaves in the flight plan? I never did think that the *Kestrel* would be able to bring off a landing if she found anything promising; but there were three ships in her vicinity that could have been diverted to any promising target she sighted, at least at any time during the next ten years —one of them the *Dart*, which is in near-perfect shape. But now that's no longer possible. And yet the one inhabitable planet that we're all seeking might very well be along that radius of expansion from home. With the *Kestrel* gone, that planet will never be discovered—not by our race, anyhow. That's what giving me nightmares."

Jorn swallowed and excused himself. There were times when the Director seemed to him to be utterly inhuman.

"What's the matter, Birn?" Ailiss said from the RF bridge, as he resumed his post. "Director dress you down?"

"Oh, shut up."

"Mind your tongue!" she said, turning quite white. "I've had about enough insubordination from you. I could use a navigator who doesn't have to count on his fingers—and by the Ghost if I get any more lip I'll go recruit me one."

"You give me a great big fat blue-green fuzzy frozen pain in my starboard rump, Apprentice-Admiral O'Kung," Jorn said, hunching forward over his desk and glaring up at her. "My math is better than yours and always was, and you know it. If you can find a better navigator, go ahead—I'd rather rub brightwork than be the kicking-boy for your twitches any longer."

"One word more, and—"

"Down, girl. If you don't like it here, go back where you came from, but *lay off me*—beginning right now. I didn't volunteer you out of your attaché's office. If I could, I'd volunteer you right back into it before you could draw another breath. Especially since it's a little bit on fire by now. But lay off—or lie down, I don't care which."

Ailiss' distorted mouth was opening and closing rapidly, but not quite completely, like a singing bird's, but no sound came from it but a sort of hoarse hiccup. This one, Jorn thought detachedly, is going to be a beauty when she finally gets it out. He didn't care. He hadn't enjoyed himself so much since he had kicked Jurg Wester out of the armorer's office; which had been—when?—some time before the last glaciation, probably.

This was the end, that was for sure. From now on they would never be able to work together again, not even by exchanging frigid monosyllables on the job and otherwise ignoring each other's existence. If they were even to try that, it would inevitably lead to a technical fiasco, and thence, if they persisted, to a catastrophe; each of them would be trying so hard to make the other look incompetent, or to inflict even deeper hurts, that the job would be perverted almost totally into a weapon. Better to give it up, before innocent people got hurt...or the *Javelin* went the way of the *Kestrel*.

All right, so be it. It was all unreal anyhow. Anything to get this obsessed young woman off his back. He hoped he would like polishing brightwork.

Ailiss opened her mouth and drew in her breath.

The control barrel rang. Then it rang again, and once more. As Jorn and Ailiss stared at each other in a fury of disbelief, the whole winking cavern began to pulse steadily with the slow, clear strokes of a pair of deep chimes.

Ailiss stood bolt upright, her eyes wide. So did Jorn.

"TO ALL HANDS," Ertak's voice boomed throughout the ship. "TO ALL HANDS. YELLOW WARNING ONE FOR PLANET-FALL. YELLOW WARNING ONE FOR PLANET-FALL. THIS IS A SIGHTING WARNING, BY COMPUTER ONLY. REPEAT, THIS IS A SIGHTING WARNING. STAND BY. STAND BY. YELLOW WARNING ONE FOR PLANET-FALL. STAND BY."

8

For a ship's computer to pick out a possibly likely system and sound a preliminary warning of this kind was not unique; it had happened twice before in the fleet as a whole—though never to the *Javelin*—but both these incidents had proven to be false alarms. All the same, since the event was novel to the *Javelin* herself, it created an almost undiluted ecstasy of excitement.

Since Ertak had issued his Yellow Warning One to all hands, the excitement was not confined to the crew. Even before human observers were able to examine in detail what the computer thought it had found, everyone on board the *Javelin* was looking at his neighbor, thinking, Maybe, maybe we have reached our unknown goal; maybe this is It.

After his first look at the tapes and at the star itself, however, Kamblin was puzzled.

"It's certainly an intensely luminous star," he said, "as most stars go—especially only three light years away from it. Its absolute luminosity appears to be about sixty, and its surface temperature is upwards of

15,000 degrees. That's by no means as big a sun as the model the computers are set to scan for."

"I don't see how they could have made a mistake," Jorn said, frowning. "They shouldn't have been fooled by so simple a thing as the comparative nearness of the object."

"Well, no," Kamblin agreed. "They're also supposed to search for planets, and the tape says this star has at least one. We have to bear in mind that very large brilliant stars, like our old one, are pretty rare, and they aren't necessarily the only type which might bear planets suitable for us. Even back home, from the lunar observatory, it was possible to detect four faint nearby stars, each of which had at least one planet-like companion; so actually planets must be relatively common."

"In other words, if the computer *has* made a mistake," Ailiss said, "we hope it's a happy accident."

"You could put it like that."

"We'll close in," Ertak decided. "But cautiously. Birn, I want a tangential approach, arriving at right angles to a radius of the total system at a distance of about a light year. Thereafter we'll spiral inward, making sure we don't miss any planets on the way; if we do make a landing, I don't want anybody on the back of my neck that I'm unaware of. Ailiss, begin to scan for patterned electromagnetic disturbances of any kind and keep at it until further orders. If the computer thinks there might be an inhabitable planet here, it may very well be inhabited as well ... Dr. Kamblin, you have that expression of mild indigestion again. Any comments?"

"Nothing serious. But at the rate this star is burning its hydrogen, it can't be much more than a thousand million years old. There's a question in my mind as to whether any of its planets can be far enough along in their evolution to support life in any form."

"That will wait upon inspection. What else?"

"I think a light year is unnecessarily far out. A sun this small couldn't support a solar system much larger than half that diameter."

"Quite so; thus we rule out starting inside a planetary orbit without being aware of it. Proceed, Mr. Birn."

By the time the *Javelin* was within a light year of the blue-white sun, the fever had percolated thoroughly through the crew and the stand-bys, and thence down to the passengers. Jorn, however, was beginning to feel familiar harbingers of letdown, which he suspected were shared by several other officers. It had now become visible that the star did indeed have planets—the computer estimated a total of ten. This was promising enough, and yet at the same time vaguely disappointing. After all, the system they had quitted had 116. All but two of those, or three counting the home planet, had been utterly hopeless from the view of human usefulness. To find so much smaller a number of planets here seemed to cut the odds for finding even one hospitable world below the point of credibility.

"Let's not prejudge the case on so little evidence," Ertak said abruptly to no one in particular. "We will see what the actual situation is very shortly. Ailiss, any detectable redundancy anywhere in the electromagnetic spectrum?"

"No, Director, just solar noise so far."

"Well, keep scanning; that's not significant at this distance. To all hands: We are now preparing to enter this system. Yellow Warning Two is now in effect."

There was the beginning of a muted stir throughout

the *Javeline*, as battle gear and drop ships began to be readied. Jorn, going for his own gear, wondered how Ertak had been so quick to detect the first faint stirrings of defeatism among his officers; on most occasions he had shown himself to be next to no psychologist at all. Maybe Ailiss had done it for him.

In any event, the die was cast. The *Javelin* was beginning her slow, circuitous drop toward the blue-white sun.

Excerpts from the Grand Log, as broadcast by the Javelin *in the course of exploration of System IEP #3:*

"The most distant planet of this system is at a distance of 6,720 million miles from its primary, with an orbital period of 610 years. It is quite dark, with some whitish streaks not parallel to its equator, its diameter is 10,000 miles and it is accompanied by two small moons. One is 250,000 miles from its primary, with a period of 24 days and a diameter of 30 miles. The second, 5,000 miles out, has a period of four hours and a diameter of three miles. It is presumed by Dr. Kamblin to be a captured comet. No landings attempted.

"The next planet inward, at a distance of 2,500 million miles, has a period of 420 years and a diameter of 33,000 miles. It is dark and moonless. No landings attempted.

"The next, obviously the first to be detected by the computer, is a gas giant of 110,000 miles diameter, at a distance of 4,500 million miles from the primary and with a period of 265 years, and close approach reveals the common methane-ammonia-hydrogen pattern for worlds of this size. It is thermally quite hot, though not self-luminous in the visible spectrum. It has six large moons, the largest 4,000 miles in diameter and with a deep but thin atmosphere, and 17 small ones ranging from 10 to 160 miles in diameter. No landings attempted on the moons as yet.

"Between this world and its nearest neighbor inward there is a wide gap which has defied explanation and presumably is responsible for the computer having described this nine-planet system as having 10 planets. The next planet is 850 million miles from its sun, 40,000 miles in diameter and with a period of 30.5 years. It is accompanied by seven small moons and one of about 3,900 miles diameter. This large moon is 800,000 miles from its planet. The planet itself presents a speckled appearance, as though it had many high, snow-clad mountain chains, although this is obviously impossible. No landings.

"The next world is a small high-albedo gas giant 450 million miles from its primary, with a diameter of 15,000 miles and period of 12.25 years. It has two small moons and exhibits the usual methane-ammonia-hydrogen characteristics. No landings.

"Inside the orbit of this world there is a highly unstable and not very dense belt of meteoric and planetary matter with wide gaps and many members which fail to conform to the orbital plane of the system as a whole. The total amount would make up a planet about 3,000 miles in diameter, and the belt probably represents such a planet, torn apart (or prevented from forming) by the gravitational force of the biggest of the gas giants. It is not so widespread as to represent a serious hazard to navigation.

"The most interesting objects in the system are twin planets, each 7,000 miles in diameter, of considerable density, and exhibiting extensive (though not chemically identical) atmospheres. One is 90 million miles from the primary and has a period of 285 days; the other is 67 million miles out and has a period of 224 days. The planet at 90 million miles is of especial interest and will be reported on in detail; the other is too hot to support life except at the poles, and even there only for half the year, as the planet has a pronounced axial tilt.

"Finally, there is a very high albedo planet with a diameter of 4,100 miles, going around its primary in 81 days at a distance of 30 million miles. It appears to have been belted into a smooth ball, and is surrounded by a slight haze spectroscopically identified as composed of vaporized metals, predominantly heavy radioactives. It is of remarkable density and has a high eccentric orbit."

There was no doubt about it now. The third world, even seen from just outside its atmosphere, was wholly inhabitable. In contrast to the second planet, the air showed no detectable carbon dioxide, and hence no greenhouse effect would exist to run up the surface temperature. Thermocouple studies showed that to be intolerably torrid all the same at the equator, all year round—for the planet had no axial tilt, and hence no seasons—but there were cool poles, and two "temperate" zones for which a better adjective would be "balmy." The spectroscope also showed the air to be somewhat low in oxygen; but in view of the prevailing planet-wide, eternal summer, this was not a real disadvantage. At least nobody on this world would have to expend any energy just keeping warm.

In any event it appears to be this one or none," Kamblin concluded. "Does anybody want to enter a demurrer?"

"Well . . ." Jorn said hesitantly.

"Yes, go ahead, Jorn."

"I've been thinking, it's kind of enervating to live where it's warm-to-hot all the time—and I think we've all had a full enough dose of hot weather over the last five years on our own planet to last us a long time. What about the biggest satellite of the giant planet? That planet radiates a lot of heat, enough so the satellite is tolerably warm around the equator even at night. And this sun is plenty bright enough to give it enough light to raise crops by—even though the days might be pretty dim to our eyes."

"Interesting," Ertak said. "I'm against it but I can't think why; it may be only emotional. Dr. Kamblin?"

"I have two objections," Kamblin said. "To begin with, the reason why that planet is hot is that it has a core of collapsed atoms, and it's generating a small amount of energy by the red giant or deuterium-hydrogen reaction." He got up and went to the blackboard, where he wrote:

$$_1D^2 + {}_1H^1 \rightarrow {}_2He^3 + \text{gamma}$$

"In fact it's not really so much a planet as it is a spoiled star, what we call a 'gray ghost.' Note the last term in the expression; it means that on any of those moons we'd be getting much more hard radiation than would be good for us, especially genetically. The other reason is, that satellite isn't massive enough to hold its atmosphere long enough to be a permanent home for a whole race. Even in a brief thousand million years, I estimate that it's lost about half of it."

"We could always migrate to the third planet when it got too thin for us," Jorn said. "But of course I didn't know about the radiation hazard; I withdraw the suggestion."

"Nevertheless, Mr. Birn, you have made an important point, even if inadvertently," Ertak said. "Where life can exist, life will arise—the forests below us now are proof enough of that—and a high radiation level means a high mutation rate and high evolutionary pressure. We had better keep a close eye on that satellite, and explore it the moment we've consolidated the present world—explore it *in force.*"

"Hmm," Kamblin said. "Very true; a disquieting thought."

"Now: The next problem is to select a landing place. We will need one big enough for the *Javelin.*"

"Excuse me, Director, but why not boats first?" Ailiss said.

"Because we have no need to be that cautious here," Ertak said. "A boat can't carry enough apparatus to make all the necessary tests; they're useful primarily for scouting actively hostile planets. The *Javelin* herself is the only laboratory at our disposal of sufficient size and resources to get a significant number of samples and process them thoroughly."

"Why risk throwing away four or five people?" Dr. Chase-Huebner agreed. "Especially when even their return unharmed couldn't be considered definitive? Landing the whole ship is a much more economical procedure in the long run."

"Very good," Ertak said. He picked up his microphone.

"TO ALL HANDS: THERE WILL BE NO YELLOW WARNING THREE. REPEAT, THERE WILL BE NO YELLOW WARNING THREE. BOAT CREWS, DECOMMISSION ALL BOATS AND ASSEMBLE AT LANDING STATIONS. YELLOW WARNING FOUR WILL GO INTO EFFECT IN ONE HOUR. ALL HANDS STAND BY FOR LANDING."

The landing site looked ideal, even after they were safely down on it. It was a broad plain beside the western shore of a huge body of water which, since it was both fed and drained by rivers, could safely be assumed to be fresh. Farther to the west there was a solid wall of virgin forest, marching unbroken for hundreds of miles into the foothills of a long and very high mountain range.

"Now we sit," Ertak said firmly. "I know everybody has his nose pressed to the ports, or would if we had any ports. But I want everyone to bear the fate of the *Kestrel* at the very front of his mind. We are going to make especially exhaustive bacteriological tests—and we are not going to miss any other tricks, either. The stand-bys will suit up and go out in rotation to collect samples; first man to disembark will be selected by lot. And nobody comes back into the ship without spending one full hour in the airlock under live steam at sixteen atmospheres, until Dr. Chase-Huebner's prepared to certify this planet as clean."

That took two weeks, and her certification was well hedged with conditions. "I can't rule out long incubation periods," she reminded the Director. "Some forms of viral cancer, for instance, take five or six years to incubate; and some bacterial diseases, like leprosy, may take as long as fifteen. But I assume that you don't expect any world to be completely free of disease—that would be demanding the impossible."

"No, of course not. What I want to rule out are galloping, uncontrollable, wild-fire plagues—like what happened to the *Kestrel.*"

"There aren't any in our immediate area," Dr. Chase-Huebner said promptly. "But warn everybody to watch out for dirty wounds. There's a soil bacterium that's close to identical with gangrene."

Ertak shrugged his titanic shrug. "Expectable. That kind of thing we can cope with. All right, ladies and gentlemen, we will prepare to pitch camp."

There was an instant clamor among the officers, which Ertak silenced, after a moment, with a sour grin and a wave of his hand.

"Calm down, please. I know everyone's got ship-board fever, but I assure you that you'll all be satisfied. We don't need volunteers; this is to be a foray in force from the very beginning. I want a fortified encampment covering roughly a hundred acres, centered on the ship herself. That will call for more work from you all than you'll find you're able to do. The passengers will remain behind for the time being, and the ship will be staffed on a skeleton basis by the stand-bys; they had the fun of being first out, now comes the time for them to pay the fee. I'll stay with them, of course; Ailiss, you're in charge of the camp itself. Prepare to disembark."

Crowing, the crew broke for their quarters and their gear.

Jorn's heart was in his mouth as he stepped off the ladder onto the actual, inarguable soil of the new world. He had not really realized how unlikely such a moment had come to seem to him. Nor had he known, ever before in his life, what it would be like to be in the midst of a wilderness. There had been none left at home, not even for the rich and powerful; everything there had been tamed, organized, put to use. Here, everything was new; they were starting over.

It was appallingly hard work, as Ertak had prophesied, but his training stood him in good stead. Despite the years of confinement in the ship, he had kept himself in reasonably good shape. Though his muscles ached abominably at the end of each day for the first week, he was never actually incapacitated, and finally his body caught the work-rhythm and fell in with it. After that there was no trouble.

And there was time, even while wielding spade or sledge-hammer or winch-handle, to look at the life around him. There were no birds here, but there were plenty of delicate insect-like creatures of many species, none larger than a hand's breadth. Often they simply hovered, with improbably slow motions of their wings; sometimes, on the other hand, they traveled with invisible speed from one hovering spot to another, slowing down into visibility only for an unpredictable swerve, and then accelerating beyond vision again. None of these seemed to have stinging or biting habits; after watching them for a long time, Dr. Chase-Huebner authorized disembarking small samples of the ship's livestock.

On the ground, the commonest form was a mollusc, superficially resembling a snail but considerably larger, and with as much apparent intelligence as a turtle; they were housed in brittle silicoid shells. They seemed to prefer crawling over pitted rocks; though they were sometimes found crossing over vegetation, it was only on the way to another rock. The plants over which they passed en route showed no signs of having been eaten—which was promising for the crops, some of which were just beginning to show their first shoots in the eternal summer.

All this was duly reported to the Grand Log. Messages poured in daily from the rest of the fleet, offering congratulations and voracious for more details. The four ships in the globe nearest the *Javelin* were decelerating under full drive; all the same, it would take them years to get here. The rest of the armada, not without jealousy, continued to expand outward.

Then came the morning when Jorn looked down out of a tree he was trimming to string wire, to find himself being watched by a demon. Yes, it could be described no other way.

It was a striped animal, four-footed, about twice as big as a man and obviously at least four times as heavy; it looked, in fact, almost overstuffed. It padded smoothly, soundlessly in figure eights around the base of the tree, looking up at him with a face whose markings gave it an expression of permanent, insane fury. Occasionally it stopped and sighed; then it resumed pacing.

Jorn hurriedly dug his lineman's cleats into the tree bole and reached for his sidearm. He doubted that he could hit the beast—there were too many branches in the way—but he was going to try. With the other hand, he swung his cheek microphone into position.

"Birn calling base camp. I'm treed by something over here. Nothing we've seen before. It's big and obviously carnivorous. I'm going to take some shots at it, but I may need help."

"O'Kung here. I read you, Birn. I'm sending a squad. Try not to damage it too much—Biology will want to look at it."

"I'll try," Jorn said disgustedly and swung the mike away. Leaning back against his safety belt, he steadied the pistol with both hands and tried to lead the animal back and forth in its pacing. It was, as he had anticipated, difficult to do; the tree bole kept getting in the way. But if he could have it in the sights just as it stopped to sigh—

It stopped and he squeezed the trigger. He did not hit it—not by several feet, at least—but the result was utterly unexpected. He watched with incredulity for nearly five minutes; and then, holstering the pistol, began to climb carefully down to the ground.

He was looking down at the colorful corpse when the cautious party from camp arrived.

They dragged it back to camp and into the improvised surgery tent, where Dr. Chase-Huebner, the ship's surgeon and the chief of biology were already set up to perform an autopsy. The beast, looking somehow smaller, was hauled up onto the table, where it lay in a peculiarly floppy position, like a child's toy.

"What a face," Dr. Chase-Huebner said. "Like a devil. What happened, Jorn?"

"I wish I knew. I know I didn't hit it. But at the sound of my gun it jumped sidewise, and landed in a tangle of those clover-like plants we've been clearing away, the ones with all the long thorns. It thrashed around in there for just a moment as though it were going to jump out, and then all at once it just —collapsed. From the noises it made, you would have thought it was suffocating."

"Very likely. Those thorns must carry some kind of nerve poison—something that blocks the breathing reflex. Odd; we've been scratched often enough by them without any apparent harm. We'll send some more samples to Chemistry—and I suppose we'd better take to wearing boots and heavy puttees until we get the results." She hefted a pair of electric shears thoughtfully, and then bent to shaving the animal's belly for the first incision.

"That was my guess," Jorn agreed. "But what puzzles me is, why should it have been so jumpy about so small a noise as my gun makes? The sighing noise the critter makes itself is almost as loud. But it jumped like it had been stung."

Dr. Chase-Huebner didn't answer. She was busy painting the shaven surface with alcohol. After a moment she took up a scalpel, and Jorn, who was inclined to be sensitive about raw innards, went back to work as quickly as his dignity would allow. Questions about the creature continued to fill his mind.

"We can take the boots off," Dr. Chase-Huebner reported at the end of the next day. "There are no alkaloids on the thorns; the plants are entirely harmless, just as we first thought. And we won't have to worry about these carnivores, either. If you can't get a fast shot into one before he's on you, stab him around the limbs or the rib-cage and you've done for him."

"I don't know," Jorn said dubiously. "You never saw him when he was alive. He looked powerful—and mean."

"I assume he's both," Dr. Chase-Huebner said cheerfully. "But that doesn't matter. You see, he hasn't got any bones. He's supported entirely by nitrogen under high pressure, in sealed tubes, thick-walled but essentially flexible. When the poor animal dodged into the thorns, his 'skeleton' got punctured in several places and the nitrogen pressure was released—some of it into the outside air, but most of it into his body cavities. He couldn't support himself any longer and smothered under his own weight. Probably that was why he panicked when he heard your gun hiss, Jorn: to him the sound of escaping gas is the sound of death. Ordinarily, I assume, he has better sense than to jump into a patch of thorns."

"That's fine," Ailiss said, but she did not sound pleased. "But I'm afraid I've got another case for you. About five minutes ago a man came swearing into the first aid station with a wounded shoulder. He didn't hear anything and didn't see anything; he was digging post-holes in an open field when it happened. But it looks to us very much as though he's been shot."

Dr. Chase-Huebner agreed. She could contribute little more, except that the missile had been quite small and of relatively low velocity—not much past the speed of sound, just enough to go on through and out the other side of the shoulder. In that the victim had been lucky, for a high-velocity missile can kill a man from shock alone, no matter where it hits him.

Two nights later one of the cattle was dead of the same cause, shot all the way through the chest. A bigger and faster missile, this time; but no other clues.

"We will make the obvious assumption," Ertak said grimly. "There are no safer ones to make. That is, that there *are* intelligent natives here after all—without electricity, but with enough brains to construct missile weapons of relatively low velocity and accuracy—and that they're keeping under cover and sniping at us. I want a doubled guard, and a twenty-four-hour infra-red watch from the bridge of the *Javelin*; also radar, sonar, trip-wires, the works. If anyone *sees* a native, notify headquarters first; I'd rather catch one than kill one."

Within a day, the camp was in a state of siege. Within a week, a woman on the agronomy team was creased lightly across the back. Two weeks later, an officer on temporary duty as a lineman, as Jorn had been when he had met the stuffed tiger, was killed, a hole driven right through his skull; it took most of the day to get his body out of the tree in which he had been working, but it did not tell them anything they did not know already. Then there was a lull, which lasted more than a month. It ended when the woman who had sustained the back crease earlier was brought in with a shattered knee-cap.

"Their accuracy," Ertak said, "is improving. And still we haven't seen a thing. From now on, the guards are to wear spacesuits at all times, day and night; the rest of you will sleep in the ship. All the animals are to be brought back in. Birn, doesn't analysis of the apparent direction of the shots give you anything?"

"No, Director, not a thing, except that we're obviously surrounded."

"Which is logical. Orders to capture a native if possible are hereby rescinded; we can't afford these losses. The new orders are: Shoot to kill."

It was almost as though he had been overheard. For nearly two months, the only incident was a minor flesh wound. One of the night guards also reported in with a bright weal across one hip of his suit, which might or might not have been the result of a grazing shot; there were no traces of extraneous metal in the weal, the steel had simply been polished. He hadn't even heard the impact, let alone felt it, and the weal wasn't turned up until suit inspection.

Then, in broad cloudless daylight, ten naked unarmed men came out of the forest to the west, and walked slowly toward the distant, bristling fence of the encampment, which was yet unaware of their action.

9

It was lucky, although it was probably also inevitable, that the natives were spotted first by the watch atop the *Javelin,* and the alert conveyed directly to Ertak. A quick, fierce look at the magnified image on his screen evidently was enough to convey to him, first of all, the absolute nakedness of the entire deputation; and secondly to convince him that if this race nevertheless had arms and could use them, the deputation was probably enfiladed by many invisible warriors in the forest behind them. His command boomed out over the camp from the *Javelin's* loudspeakers like the voice of a god:

"HOLD YOUR FIRE! I REPEAT, HOLD FIRE!"

Jorn was the first to reach the creatures, with Ailiss and her party panting not far behind. As soon as the natives saw them coming, they stopped and waited peaceably, even passively, their hands held palms outwards at their sides.

Jorn was most astonished at their absolute humanity. These were all males, and except for a certain oddness in the shape of the eyes, and a rather silvery sheen to the skin, they could well have belonged to any of the races of Jorn's own people. That they were savages seemed attested to by their nakedness, which was accentuated by a few stripes of paint on bodies and arms, all identical except for one man who was entirely without them; yet they did not give the impression of being savage—quite the contrary. Jorn's immediate impression was one of total inoffensiveness, even of timidity.

He spoke to them, and one of them to him, in a questioning voice so low that it was almost a whisper, but of course to no effect. Nevertheless, the exchange reinforced his impression that their intentions, at least for the present, were not war-like. On a hunch, he turned and beckoned, and then began to walk slowly back toward the ship.

Despite their obvious weaponlessness, he quickly developed a powerful itch between his vulnerable shoulderblades. He kept walking.

Thus, by the time Ailiss and her party arrived, all ten of them were trooping docilely after Jorn. Ailiss' party, managing to look wise, belligerent and baffled all at the same time, had no choice but to fall in around them as a sort of inadvertent honor-guard.

That they were intelligent was established almost instantly. Ailiss was able to ask them a question and get a significant answer before either party had learned a word of the other's language. After inspecting their hands quickly and finding them essentially just like hers, she included them all in a quick gesture and held up ten fingers. To this, the leader—the unpainted man who had spoken to Jorn—responded at once by pointing to Ailiss and holding up one finger, to Jorn and Ailiss and holding up two fingers, and to Ailiss' party and holding up five. Although her expression showed that she was a little stunned, Ailiss promptly included the whole of the forest behind them with a sweep of both hands, and then simply looked at the leader; to this he made a movement of his head which might have been either negative or positive, and then, seeing that she did not know how to interpret this, he held up one hand with all the fingers closed.

Ailiss turned to Jorn. "If he understands me, he means that there's nobody in the forest behind him," she said, frowning, "and damned if I don't think he does."

"I think so too," Jorn said. "Let me try it once."

At her nod, Jorn pointed to the horizon across the lake and then did a slow 720-degree pivot, returning at last to look at the leader. To this he responded with so rapid an opening and closing of both hands that it was impossible to keep count, nor did Jorn believe that that was what had been intended; it was the plainest kind of manual sign for the word "many."

"He understands, all right," Jorn said. "He's not only intelligent, but he's exceedingly fast on the uptake. I think we'd better be careful, no matter how harmless these ten may look."

"For once," Ailiss said grimly, "I couldn't agree with you more."

The party picked up the language of the people of the *Javelin* with astonishing rapidity, much faster than anyone in the camp could pick up theirs. The humiliating reason for this, it soon turned out, was that theirs was by far the richer and more complex. Among the several knots in it which nobody proved completely able to untie was a syntax of states-of-being, partly referrable to the emotions and partly to a construct of metaphysical concepts, which Ertak was not psychologist enough and Ailiss not philosopher enough to plumb more than fractionally. Nobody else in the camp ever got any farther than recognizing its existence.

But there seemed to be no reason to be afraid of them or of the people they represented. Their sole desire, and indeed the whole purpose of their visit to the camp, seemed to be to know whether the strangers in the giant house had any orders they could have the honor (sanctity? enrichment?) of obeying. Toward the end of the second week, one bold unauthorized soul among the crewmen, seeing one of the natives standing nearby watching her work, as they watched everything, with an air of interested submissiveness, took it into her head to indicate to the native that he should take over the dirtier half of the job she was doing.

The impulse doubtless came deep out of the wells of the lost past on the home planet, when she might automatically have done the same thing with the nearest passing drone. But what counted was that the native took up the spade at once and, handling it oddly but not inexpertly, proceeded to dig her her trench with great speed. He then shouldered the spade and waited for more orders—but by that time the incident had been seen by one of Ailiss' non-coms, and it was speedily brought to an end. The woman was given a dressing-down both on the spot by Ailiss and later by Ertak, but not entirely wholeheartedly in either case: the incident had been regrettable, perhaps, but after all it was also a datum.

And yet, as later, more tentative experiments showed, the attitude of the natives toward working for their guests was hard to define. They did so willingly and quickly, and yet without any apparent pleasure. It was as though they knew they had gotten what they had come for, and were satisfied to find their expectations realized, and that was all . . . "Almost," Ailiss summarized uneasily, "like a guilty man who's decided he'll feel better if he turns himself in and takes what's coming to him."

Some limited field work with the local tribe, with which the ten men of the deputation cooperated completely, confirmed and widened this impression. For all their intelligence, the natives had no technology. They had no shelters except flimsy temporary ones against rain and sun; they had almost no tools, and those that they did make were those expectable, at best, from the most refined and sophisticated era of a late Stone Age; they were nomadic hunters, dependent about equally upon fleetness of foot and fire-hardened thorn daggers. The closest thing to a missile weapon that anyone could find among them was a sling, used only against game they could not outrun.

Except for the stuffed tigers, whose fatal secret they knew with surgical precision, they had no natural enemies. They used neither thorn nor sling against each other, and seemed completely shocked at the idea after it was conveyed to them, with much linguistic difficulty. It was in fact so unthinkable that their codes contained no prohibition against it. In all other respects their social and religious structures were elaborate in the extreme, and both were buttressed by a long and equally elaborate literary tradition, mostly oral, but with key works preserved upon fine parchment in a written language which was the despair of everyone on board the *Javelin*.

And yet, trimmed of all these riches, the central tenet of their religion seemed to be that of utter resignation to anything that a completely malignant Fate might bring.

"Which is a peculiarly anomolous notion in such a paradise as this planet seems to be," Ertak said, when he was appraised of it. "And yet I don't see how it can have grown up without some reason in the real universe to give it weight. There's still some cause for caution here, which we simply haven't fathomed yet. In the meantime, I must say, in one way it seems to be promising."

"How's that, Director?" Ailiss said.

"If these people are just as we see them to be now," Ertak said, "then they appear to be an ideal work force for a more aggressive race like ours—and I needn't remind you that manpower is going to be one of our chiefest problems, even after the other ships get here. The question of slavery doesn't raise itself, happily; as far as I can see, these people seem genuinely to want to be pushed around. All right, we'll push— but gently, bearing in mind what happens to cultures who come to think that they can really own a man."

"It would make a nice stable relationship all around," Ailiss agreed. "Nevertheless, Director, I can't quite rid myself of a few misgivings."

"Oh, as to that," the Director said moodily, "neither can I."

That conference took place late one night aboard the *Javelin;* it was one of the regular monthly planning boards which had evolved more or less naturally as the camp seemed to be settling down toward a routine. Some time during the same night, one of the spacesuited guards was killed. He was pierced clean through; so was the suit.

In the ensuing consternation and fury, only prompt action by Ailiss O'Kung's squad was able to prevent the mass murder of all thirty-five of the natives who had spent the night in the compound. She was as furious, Jorn could see, as any of the rest of them, but primarily at herself, for her failure to have asked any of the natives, over the more than a month when the state of communications between them could have made it possible, if they could shed any light upon this random sniping.

"Certainly," the leader said, obviously as content as usual to find that he could be of service—quite as content, in fact, as he seemed to be over the four deaths in his party which Ailiss had been unable to prevent —but filled with wonderment at the simplicity of the question. "Those are the insects."

No one believed it at first. Yet it speedily became evident that there was something decidedly peculiar about the insects, all the same. Attempts to capture some of them were defeated in a variety of ways: first by cut nets and punctured airscoops; then by several skin creases, and eventually a serious and all too familiar hand wound. They would not be caught, and after a while it began to appear that they could not be caught.

After nearly two weeks, a small cloud of gnat-like motes was captured by the elaborate expedient of gassing it. They came drifting down through the poisonous cloud in strangely slow, erratic spirals, as though they weighed nothing—and they tinkled bouncing into the collection bottles like bird-shot.

The returns from the field laboratory showed that the natives had been telling the truth, though they were even more incredible. Under the microscope the tiny creatures proved to resemble beetles more closely than they did gnats; and their rigid exoskeletons seemed to be made of something closely resembling tool steel. The wings under those impossible wing-cases had iron-sheathed venules: and the color in the blood of the creatures was provided by flecks of rust, which picked up and lost oxygen and energy by changing cyclically from ferrous to ferric oxides and

—impossibly—back again. Nothing so heavy for its size could ever have flown, not even an inch.

They could not, indeed, be said to be true fliers, despite the wings. Instead, they hovered or travelled in the planet's magnetic field. Such wing movements as they made set up eddy currents throughout the metal exoskeleton, which were promptly transformed into movement, at more than bullet-like velocities, along a line of magnetic force. The sudden slowing and veering motions which had been observed from the beginning were probably attributable to passage over local iron ore deposits; there was plenty of the metal on the planet, though the natives did not know its uses.

"The velocities involved vary, but some are quite sufficient to penetrate a spacesuit with a man in it," Dr. Chase-Huebner reported to a hastily convened council of war. "The injuries and deaths we have sustained thus far have been due to nothing but standing in the way. We shall sustain many more, depending entirely on how long we decide to stay here. I can think of no way to prevent it, and neither can anybody else that I have talked to."

"Does the impact kill the insect too?" Jorn asked.

"Undoubtedly," Dr. Chase-Huebner said, "though that seems to me to be small consolation. And in addition I have a few other discoveries to report to you all, none of which you are going to like very much. You have all seen these brittle little molluscs with the silicon shells crawling around on the rocks. They are no joke either, it turns out. All the time we have been ignoring them, they have been crawling over the *Javelin* as well, working hard on all the ship's outside sensing instruments which have fused quartz lenses; and they have ruined about twenty per cent of them and damaged almost half of the rest. These two examples, plus that of the inflated tiger that you ran afoul of, Jorn, suddenly made a pattern in my mind and I asked the natives about it, with Ailiss to help me over the hard spots. My conclusion is that the probable and possible dangers of this kind that we will encounter if we expand over this planet are just about numberless."

"Of what kind?" Ertak said. "I can't see anything in common among the three."

"I'm not surprised, but *I* should have, long before this. In brief, Director, what has happened here is that on this planet, evolution has adopted nearly every imaginable path for giving its creatures structural rigidity. This includes both plants and animals, and a good many borderline or mixed forms; I can show you a catalogue later. *And it has also produced all the compensatory attack mechanisms.*

Some of these, like the inflated tiger and the thorn, don't represent any particular danger to us. Some of them, like the iron insects, look difficult indeed to cope with. Some of them are outright impossible: there are highly organized animals on this planet with skeletons like ours, of which the natives are the immediately available example, and natural enemies for them which are as deadly to us as the thorn is to the tiger. One of these, in fact, is a plague quite capable of turning our bones to a watery jelly in about thirty-six hours. We are only lucky that we haven't encountered it yet, especially since it never occurred to me to look for such a thing while I was making my bacteriological tests of this world.

"In short, it turns out that the native religion of complete resignation to an implacable Fate accurately reflects things as they are on this planet. The place is gay, colorful, fertile, inviting—*and wholly uncolonizable.*"

"The natives seem to get along," Jorn protested.

"The natives," Dr. Chase-Huebner said with a sad and glacial calm, "are the last tatters of their species. They will probably be extinct before ten more generations have passed. Like most intelligent anthropoid creatures, they're unspecialized in the biological sense, and under these conditions their intelligence is of no use to them. They won't have time to develop a technology sufficient to protect them. We found them here only because we arrived while their planet is still young."

"But we have the technology—" Kamblin started to protest.

"I assure you, Dr. Kamblin, that we do not. We will be unable even to protect ourselves; nor will we be able to do so after the other four ships have landed here, if we let them. I will have a full written report ready for you all by day after tomorrow; if you are not convinced now, I am fully persuaded that you will be after you have read it."

No one left the ship for the next two days, and the caves and halls of the *Javelin* were hushed with a silent fury of reading. On the morning of the third day, Ertak's voice came tiredly and heavily over the public address system.

"To all hands: Prepare to embark."

Easier said than done; relaxation of vigilance and felling of trees had spread the encampment wider and wider, and there were the damaged sensor lenses to replace too, with a squad to keep the molluscs off the ship henceforth. At Jorn's suggestion, the perimeter of the camp was drawn in to about half the distance over which the would-be colonists had been working, and the intervening space between perimeter and jungle became a sort of tunnel of charged wire, like a loosely wound armature about fifty feet in diameter. The effect was to scramble the local magnetic field so that very few of the insects could "fly" at all inside the encampment. In fact—though this hadn't been foreseen—there were soon thousands of them trapped inside the tunnel. The electrified boma consumed a lot of energy, but they had energy to spare. What was more important, hardly anyone was hurt thereafter, and nobody was killed.

The planet had one last unpleasant surprise for them, however. On the last day before embarkation would be possible, a lookout spotted a reptilian head coming along the surface of the lake toward them. As it drew closer, the head rose, on the end of an impossibly long neck and then the creature's bow wave broadened, yard by yard.

Dr. Chase-Huebner studied it through binoculars. "Something like a plesiosaur, only much bigger," she said finally. "I wouldn't like to count on the charged wire stopping it—and even if it did, that neck is plenty long enough for it to arch over the wire and grab anybody close by."

"Maybe we could order some natives to swim around behind it and stick thorns in it?" Ailiss said dubiously.

"Useless. There must be yards of blubber under that hide to keep such a monster afloat, especially in fresh water. And in fact the chest looks armored—I can't tell about the rest of it. We'll be very lucky if we can even shoot it."

"I can shoot it," Jorn said abruptly. "If I've got time." He was already working frantically at the jury-rigged exterior board which fed power to the fence. "Hey, you, drive that little truck over here—no, dammit, closer, I want to be able to reach the engine."

The monster's chest rose higher in the water, its head weaving back and forth nearly a hundred feet in the air. The shallow water churned to either side of its chest.

"It's got flippers," the lookout said. "Not legs."

"Lots of sea animals back home made fair speed overland on flippers, for short distances," Dr. Chase-Huebner said. "And a short distance is all this one needs."

Paying out wire, Jorn jumped eight of the twelve switches of the fence to the distributor of the truck's engine, which was idling. At once, the tubular gray cloud which surrounded the encampment—the trapped insects—began to move, slowly, and all in the same direction.

"It works," Jorn said with grim satisfaction. "Driver, run up the engine slowly. And keep right on running it up until it's racing, and keep it there."

The roar of the engine grew slowly. As it did, the circular cloud moved faster and faster, and from it came another roar, as of a distant gale.

Both sounds grew. The gray cloud changed color; now it was a dull red.

"Faster!" Jorn shouted.

The engine snarled. The circling cloud turned glowing white and began to scream like a cyclone. By now, of course, the insects were all dead, but their metallic cores hurtled onward in the circling magnetic field.

Then Jorn snapped off one non-jumped switch. At the lakeside, history's longest, widest, densest column of white-hot grapeshot screamed straight out of the tunnel of wire. It struck the looming saurian at an angle. Nevertheless, the monster vanished utterly. Nothing was left but boiling red water.

"Cyclotrons," Jorn said, "are useful instruments. But we'll have to board on the double, now. The screen's destroyed and the insects will be back."

10

After nearly a year on the planet, the order to embark had come with sickening suddenness, and the embarkation itself was so hasty that there was no time left any more to talk about the problem itself. The *Javelin* was driving outward from the blue-white sun at full acceleration before the four ships who had veered that way could even be told to turn back, and the reasons why so promising a world had had to be abandoned took considerable explanation to them and to the rest of the armada—and then the explanations had to be made all over again, because those who had made them the first time had been so low in heart that they had been too curt to be wholly understandable. Besides, nobody on the other ships had seen the lake creature.

And even another year thereafter, many of the captains of the other ships remained openly critical of the decision; the more boldly so since there was no way any more by which any displeasure Ertak might have felt at their criticism could be vented upon them. Though perhaps no one but Ertak sensed it at the time, it was the beginning of the end of his power as Director of the IEP and commander of the armada.

It was perhaps more important that this dissent was shared by a significant number of the people aboard the *Javelin*, particularly among the passengers, although in Ertak's own demesne the criticism was necessarily less vocal. After all, it had been a beautiful place, hadn't it? And they had never even gotten around to naming it, much less exploring and exploiting all its visible promises. Supposing it had cost them some loss of life to consolidate it? Did anyone expect anything less, on any planet they might choose to try to settle? And when, after all, are we likely to see its like again? Not until we are old, surely . . . or, perhaps, never.

The officers, in general, knew better, yet the feeling was endemic in their country too. Even after a year, they talked about hardly anything else but hindsight ways of coping with one or another of the experienced, reported or conjectured menaces summarized in the Chase-Huebner Report.

"Take the magnetic insects, for example," Jorn said privately to Ailiss. "Once the other ships had landed, we could have expanded the camp and kept up a really big electrical barrier without any significant energy drain at all."

"First of all, you couldn't put down five ships the size of ours in the same area anywhere on that planet," Ailiss said, "and even if you could, each one of them would have to have had its own camp, each with its own electrical chevaux-de-frise; I don't know what the maximum radius of protection such a gimmick would grant you, but it couldn't be very large."

"Ailiss, your answer to everything is an automatic No."

"If you'd stop pasting that sticker on my nose every time we argue, you might actually hear what I'm saying."

"All right, go ahead."

"Good. The next thing is, our intention is to colonize a planet, not just garrison it—crouching in self-limited camps which can't be expanded beyond a certain perimeter. The only real protection in the long run would be to exterminate the insects—and what that would have done to the balance of nature on that planet I don't know, but I'm inclined to think it would have created even more damage in the long run. Dr. Chase-Huebner thinks so, that's sure."

"That's true enough, but it's only one such expedition," Jorn insisted. "If that one wouldn't have done it, there are lots of others that might have been possible. After all, it's only a technical problem, and there are always solutions for those if you look hard enough."

"It's not a technical problem, it's an ecological problem, which is something entirely different," Ailiss said. "It wasn't only the insects, it was the whole planet. You can't approach a problem like that one on a piecemeal basis. Look: Supposing I grant you that we might well have come through, after years and years, even though a good many of us were killed or crippled in the process. Now you grant *me* this: supposing we didn't? No other ship has made a planet-fall yet, and the *Javelin* contains a big fraction of all that there's left of the whole of humanity. It simply isn't permissible that risks be taken with that, on nothing better than speculation and boldness. Of course some chances will have to be taken, there's no way around that and I wouldn't want to catch anybody thinking that there might be. But at least they ought to look like good chances—not just blind gambles."

Jorn could see that there was justice in this argument, which he had heard advanced before, in more condensed form, by Ertak; but nevertheless he did not feel compelled to agree with it. He was realistic enough to grant that since the die had been cast, that ended the debate, at least for this time. Next time, however—if any such situation were ever to arise again—he had every intention of raising his voice more loudly in the councils of the officers.

Neither the *Javelin* nor any other ship in the armada was ever likely to find a planet which was not hostile in some degree; and suitable planets of any kind seemed to be so scarce that chances, even blind chances, were going to have to be taken. It seemed to him that pulling up stakes every time a world showed its fangs, and going on to look for a blander one, was in itself in the long run a matter of taking the longest of all long chances with the remaining scraps of humanity . . . for after all, the search was being conducted in a limited strip of finite time, cut off at its visible end by the lifespan of man. It was nonsense to suppose, as fiction writers often had done, that the next generations might carry on the search successfully; with no experience of any other kind of life than ship life, their judgment in selecting planets to land on was bound to be bad, and their chances of being wiped out utterly by their first choice very good indeed. The chances would have to be taken by those who knew something about the odds; those who did not would fare just as well, or just as badly, by selecting their star of choice from a table of random numbers.

And as the years passed, and the *Javelin* began to bury in space, one by one, the irreplaceable members of her original complement—some of them carried off inevitably by age, some suddenly by physical or medical accident—the odds grew longer and longer. There was nothing to write in the Grand Log; and the next day, nothing again. One by one, too, the ships of the armada were passing out of earshot, even to the straining, hypersensitive nerve-ends of the Ertak Effect. The expanding, misshapen globe of ships now encompassed an unthinkably enormous volume of space, without filling that volume in the least; and the *Javelin* and her four sister ships who had stopped or slowed down for the system of the blue-white sun were the farthest behind of all, and still losing ground every day. The armada was no longer an entity, but only a loose system of far-flung outposts. Before very much longer it would cease to be even that, leaving behind only a number of single cells, each alone and silent in the voiceless night.

There were other silences, already, which were not so easily accounted for. Several ships had stopped transmitting while still well inside the theoretical reception area of the Ertak Effect. Sometimes they had simply failed to respond to calls after a short silence, then and thereafter; sometimes the broadcast was broken off in the middle of an apparently routine message; and twice the end was a garbled message, or a fragmentary one, obviously intended to be final, but impossible to interpret. In only three of these vanishments was there enough information available to construct a sensible hypothesis of what had happened to the ships, and in those three it appeared to have been a major accident of some kind—one of them a roaring, self-propagating engine-room explosion so unlikely according to theory that it shook Ertak all the way to his secret core; he promptly shut the *Javelin*'s drive down for nearly two weeks while he had it rebuilt almost from the deck-plates up, and therafter kept detailed, tape-recorded instructions for so doing spraying off into space over and over again until he had gotten acknowledgments from every ship that could hear him that the instructions had been received.

For the remaining disappearances there was no explanation at all.

Of the ships still in flight and still in range, none had yet reported a successful planet-fall, and it was apparent to everyone that the process of attrition of the fleet was far advanced. Kamblin, in a moment of reflection unusually morbid for him, extrapolated this curve: at this rate, there would be nothing left of the fleet at all within the *Javelin's* range, before the second generation would be old enough to have to worry about it, let alone be prepared to take command from its elders.

And then, to everyone's incredulity, came the hour of the death that they had been fleeing.

Had it really been that long? Jorn, looking into a polished hullplate at his graying temples, could see that it had; yet he found it hard to believe. Except for the botched colonization attempt, the years had all been so much alike since take-off that it was difficult to accept that they had been years at all.

"Everyone feels that way," Ertak said. "And that's one of several reasons why I mean to broadcast the view of the explosion over the general intercom system. I know what you're going to say, Ailiss. I remember very well that the last broadcast we got from home had a nasty emotional effect on ship life as a whole, but I'm persuaded that a good deal of time and experience has intervened, and that the people have both the stamina and the right to see the end come. Nor is it an ordinary way for a world to end; Dr. Kamblin tells me that a supernova happens in a galaxy on the average of less than once every three

hundred years. It will not be pleasant to watch, but
it will be spectacular. I for one shall take some pride
in that; I counsel you all to try to do the same."

The Sun hung there in the screens, calm, steady,
about the size of a fist. It would have looked like that,
in its present swollen state, to someone on a satellite
of the next-to-outermost planet of the home system.
Nothing seemed to be happening; but along the bottom of the screen was a thin ribbon of color, like a
tape-recorded rainbow—only the screen on the bridge
was big enough to hold all seven decks of it, for the
complete spectrum was 13 feet long—along which
vertical lines, striations and shadings shifted and shut-
tled. In the doomed star the eternal blacksmith was
forging more and more iron, more and more cobalt,
more and more nickel, more and more zinc . . .

And then, at first so slowly that the motion in the
image seemed to be only an illusion brought on by
staring, and then faster and faster, the Sun began to
shrink. Within five hundred seconds it had fallen back
to its "normal" size; within another five hundred, it
was half as big as anyone had ever seen it before.

All the heavy metal lines, and those of titanium,
vanadium, chromium and manganese, too, vanished
instantly from the spectrum. That ribbon could not
show the sudden outpouring of gamma rays; instead,
there glowed forth the malignant blue and indigo
lines of helium, so glaringly that the rest of the spectrum seemed to dim and shrink almost to invisibility.

The Sun collapsed.

For a full second it was not there at all. All that
was left was a heartbreaking after-image upon the
retina.

The screen turned white. Then, it turned black. It
was burned out. In something less than a hundred
seconds, the Sun was shining again . . . shining more

brilliantly than all of the hundreds of millions of other stars in the galaxy put together.

In the glare of this colossal torch they fled outward, disinherited.

Jorn and Ailiss were married the next day. Somehow, there seemed to be nothing else to do.

11

Disinherited they were, as finally and completely as it was possible for a people to be, short of complete extinction. Yet the ultimate irony of their situation lay in this: that after nearly fifty years of traveling, they were now three thousand light years away from home.

Were they now by some fiat of magic to stop in their tracks and look back, what they would see would be their Sun as it had always been—although not a sun any one of them nor even any of their grandparents ever could have seen. Since where one act of magic has occurred, anything is possible, add to this halt and sighting sufficient magnification to see events on the home planet; then they might be able to watch the crowning of Gol of Dobrai, a small, uninteresting and short-lived nation distinguished only by Gol himself. He had been the first king in recorded history.

And yet a backward look with the comparatively minor magic of the Ertak Effect showed what at first glance seemed to be a different segment of the skies altogether. The enormous glare of the initial explosion had died away in slightly less than a year, leaving behind a sprawling, growing cloud like a glowing cancer which seemed slowly but inexorably to be reaching after them. The interferometer showed that it was in fact expanding at the rate of 0.31 angular seconds per year; and since not even the Ertak Effect could produce absolute simultaneity between ship time and the time of an object three thousand light years away, what they were seeing on the screens was the aftermath of the explosion as it had appeared between five and six years after the event—and since that day was in fact closer to fifteen years in the past, the malignant nebula was now actually far larger than the screens could show it to be.

The central mass of the nebula, which could not be seen, but only photographed by infra-red light, was a smooth sphere. It was surrounded by an irregular, interwoven complex of filaments and jets of glowing hydrogen, brilliantly visualized through a crimson filter. The total effect was lace-like, innocently delicate and beautiful—and intensely radioactive. From this gigantic natural cosmotron, immense gusts of cosmic rays, rich in heavy primaries, fountained out into the universe at large in never-ending blasts. The boundaries of the envelope, too, were rushing outwards at nearly six hundred and fifty miles per second; the cloud was already nearly a light year across.

And at its heart, only dimly visible through the enormously rarefied inferno which writhed and seethed about it, was a steadily glowing ball hardly bigger than their vaporized home planet: a white dwarf star—the quiet and infinitely heavy corpse of their blue-white supergiant Sun.

But the Ertak Effect was seldom called upon any more, even by Kamblin. Ertak himself had retired to his quarters almost as completely as he had in the years just before take-off, emerging like a sleep-walker at intervals of six months or more to stalk along the bridge, stare at the banked instruments, the screens and the Grand Log with an expression of stunned and remote agony, and then vanish again. His meals were brought to him by a close-mouthed and apparently not very bright teen-age boy selected from among the passengers. Occasionally Dr. Chase-Huebner visited him briefly, sometimes coming out with a few orders, but more usually with nothing to say at all. After these visits, Dr. Chase-Huebner's expression was a strange duplicate of his, but it never lasted more than a few days at most. No one else had any access to him.

Jorn did not care, and neither, he suspected, did anyone else. He had his family to think about. It now included a twelve-year-old daughter named Kasi, conceived after the most protracted and solemn discussion with Ailiss had resulted in an agreement to have no children, and he devoted almost all his free time to her, with a sort of gloomy delight. He no longer thought about his duties, nor did Ailiss; they got them over with, and that was that.

In this, it was evident, they were typical. With the actual extinction of the home world, nobody on board the *Javelin* really believed any more that there was any place in the universe that was a real and tangible world for them, except the *Javelin*—unless it was Ertak himself; but it was impossible to know what he thought, and becoming increasingly harder to care. A promising sighting by the computer of the *Quarrel*, one of the few remaining ships of the armada within range, so completely failed to disturb this pervasive, self-centered apathy that there was hardly any detectable disappointment when it turned out to be a false alarm. *The sky itself a prison is*, some anonymous hand had quoted in a slantwise scrawl across one otherwise blank page of the Grand Log; and whatever Ertak might have thought of the entry, he let it stand.

Or perhaps he never saw it; for between the day when it had apparently been written in, and the expected date of his next somnambulist's tour of the bridge, the *Javelin*'s own computer once again made the control barrel clang with Yellow Warning One.

It was a shock to find something very like the old excitement singing wirily in the air of the *Javelin* again, like sympathetic vibrations in the taut strings of some invisible harp. There was no doubt that, this time, the excitement was moderately and heavily overlaid with caution; the barriers against a new disappointment were almost visibly going up in the minds and hearts of everyone; but it was still a real excitement, and Jorn was surprised to find how ready he was to welcome it. When Ertak came loping out of his hermetic quarters to pull the tapes from the computer, his eyes glowing like corpse-fires in the dark, gaunt hollows of his face, it was as though everyone in the control barrel had an instant previously been organic marionettes, now abruptly drawn together and set to dancing by the hands of their accustomed master.

"These tapes are a mystery," Ertak summarized tersely, a day later. "They're completely ambiguous. Dr. Kamblin and I are in agreement that the sun involved is somewhat *less* promising than the blue-white star we last hit was, and there don't seem to be any evident astronomical reasons for the computer's having sounded the alarm at all. All it seems to have to offer is a long series of gnomic equations in probability, which in turn seem to depend on several rhythmic functions it says the system involved exhibits—but neither Dr. Kamblin nor I can find any way to tie them to the observations we have made."

"In fact, there's more to it than that," Kamblin added. "The most baffling problem of all is that the computer seems, all by itself, to have evolved a new mathematics to handle this material, which we're finding very difficult to interpret from scratch. Though I don't understand how such a thing could be, it has all the stigmata of an original invention."

"Creativity from machinery?" Ailiss said. "That's impossible. There must be some other explanation."

"I think there is," Jorn said slowly. "I've never mentioned it before, since the evidence I had for it seemed to be so wispy. But I've been suspecting for some years now, nearly five years, in fact, that the various computers within the armada had begun to work out a sort of Grand Log of their own. Certainly we fed into our computer everything in the way of data that we could get from the rest of the fleet, but that's not quite what I mean. I think there's also been some kind of direct connection."

"A lot of machines are no more creative than one machine," Ailiss objected.

"True enough; and I think it very likely that the new mathematical system you're talking about did have a human inventor—but on some other ship, maybe one that has been out of range of us for years. There would be no reason for any of the computers to store his name, they're not interested in personalities, they just gobble up data and processes."

"Well, whoever he was, he was good," Kamblin said reflectively. "We've still got a lot to learn about this scholium, but we can already see enough of the principles on which it seems to be based to suspect that it may be a powerful tool for applications in many different disciplines—which may or may not have direct bearing on ship life and ship processes, that's one of the things we *don't* know yet."

"Which is exactly our trouble now," Ertak interposed. "Getting our teeth into this discipline and mastering it is probably going to take well over a year—and during that time the *Javelin* will have swept by the star the computer has indicated without our having been able to examine it. And this is the question that I want to raise: Are we going to take the computer's word for it, without a thorough understanding of the reasons behind the choice, and plow in to look the place over anyhow? If we do, we'll be dealing from the most original kind of ignorance, since at the moment we very frankly don't know what the computer is talking about. Any opinions? Yes, Jorn."

"Long chances are all we have left, Director," Jorn said. Carefully, he laid out his reasoning, remembered from his arguments with Ailiss back before the detonation of the Sun, and scarcely thought of since. For the most part, they still seemed to him to be as valid as ever, though they were, not to his great surprise, a little tempered by the fact of his new fatherhood. This time, on the other hand, he had Ailiss on his side—a rather better prop to his courage than the marriage-dissolved Tabath.

"Any rebuttal?" Ertak said. "No? I see no hands raised; nothing but vaguely disturbed expressions. Well, that's how I feel myself. Nevertheless, we will take the chance."

Excerpts from the Grand Log, as broadcast by the Javelin *during preliminary exploration of the system IEP #5:*

"This appears to be a rather tightly organized eight-planet system whose original supply of hydrogen separated out from the primal cloud rather earlier than is usual in the formation of new stars, forming a thick shell inside which the sun involved eventually condensed. This event was evidently very ancient, since the sun is a second-generation star, implying high stability; and preliminary studies indicate that it will last in its present phase without significant change for at least another 2,000 million years—probably longer.

"The result of this accident, whose causes can now only be conjectured, is that the three outermost planets of the system are all gas giants of about equal size, widely separated in orbital distance from each other, and all so far away from the central sun that even the largest bodies among their considerable families of satellites cannot maintain atmospheres in gaseous form. An exception may have to be made for the largest satellite of the innermost gas giant, a body about 3,500 miles in diameter, which may still have a very thin atmosphere of neon and other noble gasses, but observation shows that the remainder of its original envelop now lies frozen on the rocks.

"All five other planets in the system are relatively small, dense bodies drawn close in to the sun, the outermost orbit of this interior system being at a mean distance of 300 million miles from the primary, and the innermost at about 42 million. By virtue of their surprisingly different diameters and densities, all but the innermost of these worlds appear to be habitable in some degree, and even the innermost—hot and stormy though it obviously is—cannot entirely be ruled out as an abode of indigenous life. The outermost, a body about 10,000 miles in diameter and rich in both water vapor and carbon dioxide, exhibits a frost-line after midnight almost as far down as the equatorial belt, and it is permanently glaciated in both its northern and its southern sixths; but the temperatures at noon range from hot along the equator to freezing at about 25° N. and S. latitude. As a result the prevailing planetary weather may be described as violent, but by no means intolerable.

"The three planets bracketed by these two extremes are all livable, and in fact the spectroscope shows that life has arisen on all three. The fourth planet outward from the sun, a world 9,000 miles in diameter with one very large moon and two small ones, is particularly verdant, and close inspection shows that both the planet and the large moon were in fact occupied at one time. The lunar installation is a featureless metal dome. The planet can be seen to bear many large stone and metal artifacts suggesting cities, now obviously quite silent and deserted. Pending exploration, their age, origin and fate remain conjectural.

"We are not yet able to say upon what basis our computer selected this extraordinarily promising system, but hope to accumulate more data after planetfall. Stand by."

The hammer fell. As the *Javelin* began to settle complacently into the outermost reaches of the atmosphere of that abandoned, incredibly rich planet, the smooth, blown-steel, pilot-fish shapes of the blind little ships came raining down around her out of the blackness, spitting needles of white fire. The computer rang all its bells at once, radio heat red orange yellow green blue indigo violet ultra-violet X-ray and panic, but it was too late. Above the bubble ships which were seeing to it that the *Javelin* continued to go down, turret-bumpy forts as big as small moons crashed into orbit out of nothingness, indifferently forcing the entire metrical frame of local space-time to bear their malignant tumorous masses with groans profound enough to be heard, should anyone with ears for gravitational waves be listening, almost to the center of the galaxy.

The computer yelled its mechanical horror so loudly in the control barrel of the *Javelin* that it was almost impossible to think. After a brief moment of fury and bafflement, Ertak cut its power; and then, for thirty seconds of ringing, desperate silence, he turned his back on the barrel and pressed his temples with the heels of his hands.

"We are fordone," he said at last in a high, white voice. "We will maintain our landing trajectory. We have no other choice. Ailiss!"

"Great Ghost. Yes, Director."

"Try to raise someone out there. Find out what they want; try to convince them that we're harmless. They've got us—there's no other way out."

There was no doubt about that. The hull of the *Javelin* was banging continuously with the admonitory small shot from the bubble ships, obviously not intended to wound the great clumsy interstellar vessel much, but only to see to it with a fusillade of whip-cracks that she came to ground conveniently near her proper cow-barn. She could no longer see the landing place she had picked for herself; suddenly the quiet atmosphere into which she had been settling was aroil with black storms, blinking and bursting with gigantic, jagged lightning-bolts.

"No," Ailiss said, in a hoarse whisper. "Oh, no."

The beautiful black creature on the screen smiled at her, but without mercy.

"And why not?" he said, in a voice as deep and rich as that of an organ. "You cannot say no to us. You never could. You were stupid to try; and now it's far too late. Too bad—anywhere else, you might have gotten away with it."

As Ailiss swallowed and attempted to muster an

answer, he burst into a peal of musical, glistening black-and-white laughter. There was no humor in it, though there was a great deal of joy: it was the amusement of a demon, part delight, part calculation, and part the compulsive whicker of insanity.

While the laughter died away, they had time to realize that this tall black man-thing without lashes, brows or hair which glittered at them from the screen like volcanic glass spoke their language as fluently as through he had been born to it—and as contemptuously as though he had picked it up entirely just yesterday afternoon.

"You're making a mistake," Ailiss said, with the sudden prim severity of a schoolteacher. "We're not doing you any harm."

"No, indeed. Nor will you. We've been listening to you talk to yourselves ever since your probe picked us up; we know what's on your mind—and we know about your other starships waiting outside. We mean to make an example of you. This system is *ours*."

"They may wind up making an example of *you*," Ailiss said, seizing instantly upon the slight apparent error. "For that matter, we are not as helpless as you think. We could very well plant nuclear bombs in a good many of your cities before we're forced down."

"The cities are empty," the black man said indifferently. "Do you know why you didn't detect us until now? We evacuated this planet completely when we heard you coming, and shut down electromagnetic activity throughout our system. If your main force looks too strong for us, why then we won't be found; and if it isn't—"

Symbolically he cut his throat, with a gesture all the more shocking for its complete—and completely spurious—familiarity.

Ertak, out of sight of the screen, beckoned to Jorn,

motioning for silence. Jorn walked over to him, and tried to understand his pointing finger and odd gestures. Kamblin understood first, and once he fumblingly began to carry out the action, Jorn could see what was wanted: a jury-rigged "take-off" sequence without benefit of the computers. It looked like sheer suicide, but there was no time to argue; he could no more successfully rig such a thing than Kamblin could. He buzzed crew's quarters for the armorer; she seemed to arrive almost before he took his finger off the button. She looked once, nodded once, and got to work.

"I can see that you don't have an interstellar drive of your own," Ailiss' voice went on. "You'd be better off dealing with us, instead of shooting at us. We may have a good many other things you might want."

"An interstellar drive is of no use to us," the black man said. "And if it were, we would invent it ourselves. I demean myself by talking to a race that could make such an offer. Death and destruction to you all."

The screen went dark. Ailiss wrung suddenly trembling hands.

"Ailiss, no time now for shock reactions," Ertak said in a voice as bleak as lava. "Come here and see what we're doing—and don't say anything aloud about it. I don't know whether our friend can overhear us when we're off the air or not, but I don't want to take any chances. Do you understand this rig?"

"Mmmm . . . yes, Director."

"All right, it's your job to run it, understand? Just as you would a more conventional thing of its kind. Pick your own, uh, target, and don't stint—do you follow me?"

"Yes—but—"

"I know all the 'buts' just as well as you do," Ertak

said. "We've got no time for them. You've got fifteen seconds to familiarize yourself with the apparatus, starting *now*." He snatched up a microphone. "TO ALL HANDS. THIS IS BLUE WARNING FOUR, OTHERWISE UNSPECIFIED. SEARCH YOUR MEMORIES. SIGNAL BLUE IN TEN SECONDS. SIGNAL BLUE IN TEN SECONDS."

Those ten seconds seemed preternaturally quiet to Jorn, despite the screaming of the atmosphere and the clangor of the missiles against the hull. Five . . . four . . . three . . . two . . . one . . .

With a rasping roar from the drive, more thunderous and ugly than any sound it had ever made before, the *Javelin* rolled on her axis and clawed skyward, on full emergency acceleration.

The nearest fort got off a shot at her as she passed, already doing 200 miles per second and building more velocity every instant. The shot was a clean miss—luckily, for a few thousand miles to starboard-and-rear some metallic bit of meteoric trash triggered its proximity fuse and it blossomed out into a megaton fusion explosion.

But from now on, for a while, the *Javelin* would be an increasingly better target. If the black creatures had a drive fast enough to enable them to colonize all their planets economically, furthermore, there would still be a considerable gauntlet to run.

The gabble of venom and fury spewing after them by radio did not suggest that the creatures would simply be glad to see them go. The ranging shots were coming closer—

But in fact the battle was effectively over. Had the fifth planet not been on the other side of the sun at the time, the outcome might have been different;

but as events actually fell out, there was only a stern chase, in which the *Javelin* proved to have the advantage all the way. The ranging shots fell farther and farther behind; and then, finally, they stopped.

"Radio silence until we pass the light barrier," Ertak ruled, mopping his brow. "And we'll keep the computer off, too. I strongly suspect that those devils could overhear it thinking, if they could pick up its probes from three light years out—and if it *is* in some sort of contact with computers in the other ships, so much the worse. After we pass light speed, we'll risk using my communicator to pass the word, but not before."

He turned toward his quarters, steadying himself with one hand against a bulkhead; suddenly he seemed to be all gone at the knees. Jorn could well understand why; he was grateful that he himself was already sitting down.

Then, surprisingly the Director turned back.

"Masterly piloting, Ailiss," he said. "And not as rough as I expected; but Doctor, you'd better check around for injuries. Jorn, you'd better find out where we're headed."

And then he vanished.

Her drivers still snarling under the maximum emergency overload, the *Javelin* raced outward from her second defeat.

And this one, Jorn sensed dimly, was crucial. It would never be completely forgotten; eventually, if any of them survived, it might retreat into the mists of mythology, but it could never be expunged from the racial memory. It was one thing to be driven off a verdant world by blind natural forces ... and quite another to be scourged away with whips and con-

tempt, by a people very like their own—whose last
words had been a promise of undying hatred for so
long as any member of either race remained alive. It
was a heavy blow.

12

In this Jorn was both right and wrong; for he did not know that they were not done biting that bullet yet. It was over, as far as he was concerned, when the defeat had been recorded in the Grand Log, in terms as unemotional as possible, for the benefit of the few ships that were left who could still take part in that communal rite.

Staring into the plotting tank only five years later, he saw with hypnotic gloom how few their numbers had become: only nine, counting the *Javelin*, of that original thirty-one.

Watching the tank had become one of his main hobbies these days, especially since Kasi had become a teen-ager, and become abruptly both incomprehensible and—he could hardly bear to admit it—a little hateful. He had set the tank up originally on the pretext that it would be an aid to navigation; there was nobody to say him nay, especially since time, power and materials for it had been plentiful, but it had in fact never been of much use. More recently, he had begun to entertain the faint hope that it might offer some clue to the disappearances.

That was about all there was to see in the tank: lights winking out, faster and faster—much more rapidly, in fact, than even tottering old Kamblin's original extrapolation had predicted. It seemed to Jorn that the positions and rates of the disappearances might yet reveal some pattern, and thus re-infuse at least a faint shade of meaning into the scraps and ghosts of the armada. But the few arcs and chords of the original sphere that were left for the plotter to work on were too scattered to provide sufficient data; and now the tank was only one more well-spring of despair, with Jorn hanging over it like an impotent god, waiting year after year for another world to dim and go out.

"Why do you keep watching that thing?" a dry, whispery voice said behind him. He straightened, cautiously—he was a little creaky lately. The voice was Kamblin's, of course; he had been the last of the officers but Jorn to lose interest in the tank, but lose it he had, finally.

"I don't quite know. The Ghost knows I don't have any hope of seeing anything significant in it any more. But it fascinates me, somehow."

"I can see that," Kamblin said. "I suppose I can see why, too. But I can't stand it any more myself. It depresses me too much."

"Well, I'm beyond that, maybe. I don't know... Ailiss tells me you were in to see the Director this morning. Any news?"

"No good news," Kamblin said, twisting his mouth wryly. "I'm afraid he's not going to be with us much longer."

"I suppose you're right, but it's hard to believe— I thought he'd last forever. Why, he's younger than you are ... and he's had these fits of being in isolation before. He always comes out, when there's any real need for him."

"He's a sick man," Kamblin said heavily. "Sick in his mind. This business with the black devils ... well, of course, you don't know the whole story."

"I was there," Jorn said, a little huffily.

"That's not what I mean. I don't suppose there's any harm in your knowing about it now. You see, those creatures were never there at all."

"Never there ... ! Excuse me, Dr. Kamblin, but they made some remarkably real dents in the *Javelin*."

"I know. Let me begin at the beginning. Didn't it strike you that that black man was more than a little insane, going to such lengths to destroy one ship, and refusing even to consider that we might have something to offer him? And he was the only one of them we ever saw; he made decisions that only the chief person of the entire system could have made—but under what circumstances would such a personage be in direct command of a fleet?

"Then there was his claim that they had evacuated a whole planet, in something under six months, just to trap one ship—ours. Not very easy, or very logical either. But he also claimed that they had maintained strict electromagnetic silence from the moment they overheard our computer until the time they jumped us. Tell me, Jorn, is that possible?"

"Well, with chemical rockets ... but then there's communications, logistics ... No, you're right, it isn't possible. No electromagnetics, no evacuation."

"Very good, now we reach step two: To maintain a high energy civilization, you *must* have power—lots of it. Yet he claimed that they shut themselves down entirely for six months in order to hide themselves from us; and he said they would do it again if our imaginary 'main body' proved to be too big for them to handle. For how long could they have done that? Supposing this main body had decided to stick around indefinitely? Would the black people have just remained in hiding, living on roots, until they froze to death? Not very likely."

"Hmmm. But the electromagnetic silence was perfectly real; we sampled continuously, and never heard a whisper, beyond whatever it was that the computer first picked up."

"Right," Kamblin said solemnly. "The silence was real; therefore the high-energy civilization was not. You *can't* shut a high-energy civilization down that far without exterminating it, it's just plain impossible. And if Ertak hadn't cut the power to the computer when we were attacked, we might have found that out in time. That was one of the things the computer was ringing its alarms about; it detected right away that the entire attack was being directed from a single central source—that big metal dome on the large moon. Now it makes sense, you see: you *can* shut down the energy output of a single installation to a trickle, and shield the trickle, except for detectors; and if the detectors are transistorized they don't make enough noise to be overheard from space.

"And once we turned the computer back on again and fed the tapes of the attack to it, it immediately identified the broadcast of the black man as coming from the same source. Furthermore, it identified the black man himself as a solidigraph—a construct. So we never really saw even *one* black man; we saw a synthetic image, and heard a synthetic voice. The computer also says that what was actually doing the speaking—the being with which Ailiss was really talking—*was itself a computer.*"

"Great Ghost," Jorn whispered. "But, couldn't there have been—"

"A real such race? Yes, we think so. But there are two more things to be added. While we were in our aborted landing orbit around that planet, we were photographing continuously, as a matter of course; and the pictures show that all the cities over which we passed were in a fairly uniform stage of ruin. Secondly, we passed over the spot which later turned out to be the place where our attackers wanted us to land; and after this matter came up, we examined that site closely.

"It evidently had been a landing field, a large space-port, at one time in the distant past. It's completely overgrown now, and you can only see its bare outlines. You can also see two wrecks. One of them is about three hundred years old, if we have interpreted the vegetation around it correctly. It looks rather like the *Javelin* in general design. The other one is such a ruin that almost nothing can be told about it, except that it's of completely different design. I would like to guess that the more recent of the two might have been a refugee from the Great Nova, but of course, that's just my romantic nature speaking.

"Given this much, however, we can put the story together. The black race obviously was real, and it was probably just as proud and hostile as was the ghost of it we encountered—after all, the computer involved had to build its solidigraph *and* its social attitudes from stored data, it couldn't invent them. Maybe the race was visited by an interstellar squadron once, and was sufficiently panicked to fortify against any such visitor again; so they built the lunar station, equipping it to act the moment it detected an intruder, long before the people themselves could.

"After a while—who can guess how long a while?—

the computer malfunctioned. It went mad, if you like. It decided that the black race itself was the invader against which it was instructed to act, and it so acted. If each of the two wrecks we saw was a refugee from a separate supernova explosion, as we are, then that race has been dead at least six hundred years, and probably more. The cities are in poor enough shape to support that estimate. But the trap is still there, and it very nearly made us its third victim—or, counting the black race, its fourth."

For a while Jorn could think of nothing to say. At last, he found one unanswered question:

"So then if we'd just bombed that lunar installation —but how long ago did you find this out? Wasn't there any other ship nearby who could have gone in there and done what we failed to do? It would be easy enough to pretend to walk into the trap, and then hit the lunar station with a fusion salvo—and after that, that whole beautiful system—"

"Yes, I know," Kamblin said. "That's what's hurting the Director's sanity. He could have sent a message to the *Quarrel*; she was still close enough, though we weren't any longer.

"But he didn't. And now it's too late. We lost our opportunity."

The story, like a worm at the heart of a fruit, gnawed incessantly at Jorn, for no reason that he could put his finger on. It was tragic, surely—not only for them, but for the earlier explorers, and even for the black race, for whom Jorn could now feel nothing but pity. But none of this explained why he woke up, day after day, with the awful feeling that he had somehow missed the point.

It was a dream that gave him the clue: a peculiar nightmare, more depressing at first even than the nightmare of daily living because of its apparent meaninglessness. He had had similar ones before. As when, he was about to graduate from engineering school, and facing one last comprehensive test in some subject—just which one he could not afterwards say, if indeed it was identified in the dream at all—and realized suddenly that he had never, during the entire course, paid the least attention to what the teacher had said, or even opened the book; in fact, he could not specifically remember ever having attended a class. At this he sat bolt upright, banging his forehead against the bottom of Ailiss' bunk, and said hoarsely:

"The computer!"

"Uhm? Whassa?"

"Nothing. An idea. Sorry."

By the end of the next morning the plotting tank had finally ceased to be an old man's toy. With the aid of Sergeant Strage, the aged but still incredibly deft armorer, he had wired its output end into the computer, with specific shunts to that section of the insensate brain where the new mathematical discipline was stored. Then he sat back and waited it out.

He did not have to wait long. Within half an hour the computer was showing more activity than had been evident since the disastrous retreat from the dead devils; and within an hour after that, it uncoiled a long tongue of tape which Jorn's trembling hands nearly tore in two as he tried to look at it.

For the merely human brain studying it, several weeks were required to see what the machine was driving at; during the last stages, Jorn had to enlist Kamblin's knowledge of the recondite mathematical scholium.

"No doubt about it," Kamblin said at last. "This changes a good many things—and not for the better, either, as usual."

"Well, let me be sure *I* understand it," Jorn said intensely. "The computer says that the extinction rates for the lights in the tank were higher in the wave-fronts of the fleet that were proceeding inward, toward the center of the galaxy. Correct?"

"I'm afraid so. Of course, there's a little uncertainty—"

"Uncertainty, my eye! I mean, uh, sure, it's far from obvious just from watching the spots of light in the tank, otherwise I might have seen it myself; but isn't that what the equations say?"

"I have to agree."

"All right, now: If that means anything at all, it means that the galactic center is not only a center of population for suns, it's a center of population for people. Of course, the equations don't say *that*, but how else can you account for such heavy losses? And that's the way the *Javelin* is going now. It looks to me like it would be a damn good idea to change course. Let's see what the Director thinks."

"I doubt very much," Dr. Kamblin said, "that you will ever find out what the Director thinks. But I agree that we'd better ask for some extra heads in discussing our next move."

They did not find out what the Director thought; he did not appear; Dr. Chase-Huebner, now shockingly white and withered, spoke for him. Jorn spoke for himself, but the agreed strategy called for Dr. Kamblin to open.

"So much for the facts," Kamblin was saying. "Now we are thrown into the realm of deductions, and from there into the realm of inferences. To begin with, obviously as one goes inward toward a center of population—stellar or otherwise—one's chances of locating a habitable planet begin to rise. They go up pretty sharply toward the tail of the curve, because the stars at the heart of the galaxy seem to average about a light year apart, or only a little more. If everyone is clear about this so far, I will yield the floor to Jorn Birn."

There seemed to be no questions. Jorn rose slowly. All eyes were on him.

"What I want to point out is this," he said. "The farther we go toward the galactic center, the more likely we are apt to meet more advanced, civilized, colonized, dangerous systems; the more likely we are to meet someone like the black men and get thrown out, probably with more damage. Sergeant Strage tells me that the *Javelin* can no longer survive such a fight. It's my opinion that we never could have. We lost the first one we got into so decisively that we're going to have to face up to our own pretensions. All the military training and weaponry and gimmickry, all our postures of ferociousness, look now to have been nothing but whistling past an obvious graveyard—an illimitable one, but all the same a graveyard."

"That may mean something," Dr. Chase-Huebner said, "or it may be just oratory."

"I'm not the orator type, as you know full well after all these years. Look at the facts. We proceeded from the start from an assumption—maybe a buried assumption, but all the same it was there—that we might be able to take over an inhabited planet by force. Back then, we had the temerity to think that we might find a world resembling the Akimisov Empire, big, rich and pre-scientific, that we could push over with determination and a few hand-grenades.

"The real fact of our existence, as these equations *prove*—I'm not so cautious as Dr. Kamblin—is that our whole armada is nothing but a small guerrilla force of nomads, advancing steadily farther into the heartland of cultures far older and bigger than ours. Most of the races that we meet there will probably be able to blow us all away, with nothing more than a huff or two of surprised contempt."

"Or swallow us up," Ailiss said surprisingly. "Jorn, if you don't mind, perhaps we ought to pause here for a debate on the desirability of being swallowed by a more advanced culture?"

"I've already been swallowed once," Jorn said grimly. "So have we all, and here we sit in the bowels of that very whale. I'm frank to say that the novelty has worn off, and I'm not anxious to be swallowed again by something whose very nature I can't even guess."

"Part of the fleet is going to be swallowed in any event," Kamblin noted, with a faint grimace. "And we can only hope that at least some of these disappearances in that direction mean that the ships involved were swallowed whole, without having been chewed to bits first. I can't say that I opt for that either, Ailiss."

There was a short silence.

"Well, then," Dr. Chase-Huebner said, "what is your alternative, Jorn?"

"There's only one: to turn the ship out of what's left of the armada—that's only a direction now anyhow, not a body of anything—and resume cruising along the galactic spiral arm our old Sun belonged to ... just as the Director started us out to do. We aren't out of that arm yet, of course. The stars will be sparser there and the chances of finding a good planet-fall correspondingly smaller; but all the same I wouldn't take us even one light year farther in toward the galactic center."

"I oppose it," Dr. Chase-Huebner said. "There are penalties to pay for such a policy which I don't think you have considered. If we adopt it, we divorce the

Javelin quite finally from the organism of which it is supposed to be a part . . . and I don't mean just from the remaining tatters of the physical thing, I agree that that's only a wraith now, but also from the very notion of being any longer a part of such an organism. That would deprive us of our last cultural tie with home and race, weak though that admittedly is. The results in terms of morale would be disastrous; it would, I think, destroy us."

"My field," Ailiss said. "And I disagree. Those ties are already illusory; and the second generation will not feel them at all. Look around you, Doctor; we are not young any more! That generation is treading on our heels and ought to be given its chance. It's not much of a chance, perhaps, but we are not empowered to commit suicide for them; that is their decision to make, not ours."

"Suicide is an inflammatory term," Dr. Chase-Huebner said.

"Murder is an even more unpleasant one, Doctor. I thought you would appreciate my avoiding it."

"Exactly," Jorn said. "I haven't heard anybody arguing with the computer's equations, or with Dr. Kamblin's interpretation of them. That's where we have to start. They are both perfectly definite and don't permit of any argument. All the rest, I am afraid, is emotion —as is signalled by the fact that we have already degenerated into using loaded words. And I cannot impress upon you too strongly that every minute we spend now brings us closer and closer to that enemy, whoever he may turn out to be, who will burst our bubble for good . . . and our children's as well."

Dr. Chase-Huebner's lips thinned; it was obvious that she thought she was being reminded that she had no children aboard.

"Very well," she said remotely. "I will present your opinions to the Director."

"Please," Jorn said, as gently as he could. "That's not quite how it goes. Please present our *decision* to the Director."

Ailiss' eyebrows shot up, but she offered no protest. Her old back as straight as a spear, Dr. Chase-Huebner walked away from them and into the Director's quarters. The door closed.

They waited all day, but she did not come out. The next morning, the middle-aged "cabin boy" found the door locked.

But by noon of that day, in response to some extension of control into the cabin which no one had suspected even existed, the *Javelin* began to turn.

The signals in the plotting tank faded precipitously, and went out. At last, among the miniature symbols of stars, there were only two ship lights left: The *Quarrel*, and the *Javelin* herself.

But at least, Jorn told himself, it had been by their own decision ... not only because of some failure of the Ertak Effect generators, or by some increase in the malice of the absolutely unknowable, but by deliberate action of the *Javelin*'s own crew. It was all but over; the umbilical cord had been cut.

Kamblin joined him beside the tank.

"What do you think will happen to them?" Jorn said.

"I have no evidence to go on," Kamblin said in a quiet, distant voice, as though he were half asleep, or very far away. "From now on, Jorn, it's going to be all guesses and dares ... and we're a little old for either."

"Ertak wasn't too old."

"No. More power to him. I didn't really believe ... well, no matter now. As for the fleet, about half of the remains of it is still proceeding inward—toward almost certain encounter with some kind of interstellar empire, if you and I are right."

"You adopt my view, then."

"I have to. As for the rest ... well, they are doubtless proceeding outward toward the galactic edge, and before they get there they will have to cross the Rift —a term I won't explain, it almost stops my heart to think of it. They will find no promising stars there, that's all that needs to be said. They will probably not even get to the other side. Of course, some few ships like the *Javelin* may still be cruising along the spiral arm, in diametrically opposed directions, by accident or even by policy. But if they are, it's something about which we can't know now, and will never know. The distances have grown too great; the end of the fleet as an organism is almost complete. The *Javelin* is on her own."

Together, they stared down into the plotting tank, the little lights in it glinting on the wet curves of their blind eyes.

While they watched, the point that was the *Quarrel* turned slowly russet, and then crimson. It began to dim.

For a moment, then, it brightened to a sullen orange. As a visible signal the little light had gone out, but the computer was reporting that it was still maintaining the pip in the infra-red. Now it was crimson again: a signal in radio in the tank, but growing longer and longer in wave-length ...

It flickered, turned sooty, and was gone.

The old men stood like statues over the tank for an indefinite length of time. No one seeing them could have told for certain whether they were alive or not, except perhaps by the two tears standing under Kamblin's eyes.

Behind them, at last, there was a fumbling sound;

and then an uncertain sliding of metal against metal. They turned slowly and looked up at the bridge.

Ertak's door was half open; a little light, steamy and dim, spilled out of it into the control barrel and cast itself into the plotting tank, making faint glints among the little, hair-fine wires which guided the fields in that compact planetarium. It turned Kamblin's face into a skull.

Ertak was moving along the bridge, with the utmost care. He was so thin that his joints inside his ancient, tissue-paper uniform seemed far larger than the shafts of his limbs. High on his agony-bent back the hump rode, exuberantly strong, pulling at his arms as though demanding him to help himself. In contrast, he seemed to have no belly left at all.

Somehow he reached the lectern by the communications desk where the Grand Log was kept. He looked down at it for a while, breathing heavily, but without seeming to see or to care what was written there. Then, pulling all his wobbly parts together, he lifted it, and carried it clutched to his collapsed chest, by inches, into his stateroom.

They could hear him sobbing for breath. Just as obviously, he could not.

The door closed, and they heard the slight sound of the lock. Then, with a dead slam, they heard the Grand Log fall to the deck.

None of them ever saw it again.

13

Jorn was playing Castles with Ailiss in the dimness of their cabin when the chimes began, soft with distance but quite clear. He paid no attention, nor, as far as he could see, did she. Almost all of the remains of the original crew had cabins now, thanks to the fact that the differential birth rate on the *Javelin* was negative —or, to put it another way, that there were fewer births than deaths—and the privacy was all the more valuable for the many years that they had been without it.

Not that Ailiss was much more than an indifferent player of Castles; she could think as many moves ahead as Jorn could when she wanted to, but she was given to impulses, and she had never bothered to study the classical openings and the Great Games; but with Kamblin dead, there was nobody else on board Jorn cared to play with. This time, for a wonder, she was putting up a passable resistance.

Besides, the dim light was grateful, a privilege in itself. The children were welcome to the glare of the working areas and ward-rooms of the *Javelin*; they had been born to it and seemed to prefer it, but it was hard on old eyes.

It was Ailiss' move. After a while, her mouth pursed in an expression of annoyance.

"I can't think," she complained. "Isn't that thing ever going to stop?"

"Probably. It's not our job to answer it. You're in double jeopardy, let me remind you."

"I see that. I just keep losing my train of thought, with those bells jangling away. Let's declare a recess. Maybe we ought to see what the trouble is, anyhow."

"If there's any trouble, the Director will let us know," Jorn said ponderously. "It's probably just some routine thing. Let the kids handle it, it's good practice for them."

"Jorn, my dear, how long has it been since you last saw the Director?"

Jorn frowned. It seemed an irritatingly minor question. "I can't say. Several years."

"Has it occurred to you that he might be dead?"

"Frequently. However, there have been meals coming in and going out of there all that time, and *somebody's* been eating them."

"That could be the doctor. Anyhow, I think we ought to go to the control barrel and take a look. Unless my memory has gone bad entirely, that's Yellow Warning One we're hearing."

Jorn sighed and pushed himself carefully back from the board. "I hope not," he said; but he followed her out, all the same, wincing as the fluorescent light came pouring through the open door.

They shuffled toward the barrel, favoring their individual arthritides with the unselfconsciousness of long resignation. Looking at the ship around him closely for the first time in many months, Jorn found good reason to renew his wish that no planet-fall was being foreshadowed. It was not only that he personally had been disappointed more than often enough already—he could still, he told himself, see the course of that apathy dispassionately for what it was. But in addition, the *Javelin* was shabby. The children had been keeping her running, at least as far as her essential services were concerned, but they had not been keeping her up . . . and where little negligence are allowed, big ones are sure to come creeping after, unnoticed until it is too late.

Well, perhaps that's our fault, too—all of us on the original crew. They never had the training we had. We were too old and tired and discouraged to give it to them, even if we'd had all the facilities. And of course, you can't expect anything of passengers . . .

The thought faltered. It was hard to bear in mind that there were very few passengers any more. They had outnumbered the crew enormously at the start, he seemed to recall. But somehow they had failed to breed, in anything like sufficient numbers. Odd, when you thought about it; what else had they had to do?

There were not very many people in the control barrel, and of these Jorn and Ailiss recognized only two: their daughter Kasi and her new husband, a hard-voiced, cock-sure youngster whom Jorn could barely stand. Ailiss seemed to be able to put up with him a little better, if only for Kasi's sake. He had been in training to be Kamblin's replacement at the time of the latter's death, but how much astronomy he actually knew was an open question. Hearing him talk, in that arrogant, know-it-all voice of his, Jorn sometimes got the fleeting impression that he did not think of stars as being real objects at all, but only dots with certain arbitrary properties which he had been forced to learn by rote. His name was Monel.

He did not appear to be so cock-sure at the

moment, however. Like everyone else in the barrel, he was standing at his post but not doing anything, his glance going from the door of Ertak's quarters, to the computer, and back again to the door.

The door did not open.

"How long has this been going on?" Jorn demanded.

"About five minutes, Father," Kasi said.

"That's already too long. If the Director doesn't appear in another five, we'll have to take action ourselves." The decision came out with great reluctance; but anything was better than this agony of suspended doubt, ringing with the chimes of the computer.

"And then?" Ailiss said.

"I don't know. I suppose we'll have to break into the cabin, just to make sure that he's dead . . . that they're both dead."

As an afterthought, Jorn started to cut the bells from the computer, and then, remembering the last time such a step had been taken, decided against it. Better to give Ertak, or Dr. Chase-Huebner, every possible opportunity to hear them, if they were going to within the time limit.

The bells chimed away at the minutes. At last Jorn said, "All right," and cut off the sound. "Somebody get a drill."

The whirring cutter bit into the tough metal of the bulkhead. It was heavy work; in seconds the business end of the tool was white hot. The boy wielding it sweated over his work, frowning with absurdly fierce concentration, his teeth slightly bared. After a while, he had a quarter-circle cut around the main dog, the one which carried the lock. He paused to push his wet hair back out of his eyes.

The annunciators cleared their throats, all at once. Jorn started and looked up, automatically.

"Rrch. Rk. Tsu arr hamds. Rk. Arr hamds. Yerrow Warming. Wum. Rk. Yerrow Warming Ome."

The sound sputtered and popped, and then the carrier hum cut off again. Everyone turned to look at Jorn, but he had no answers; no more did Ailiss.

The voice had been a little like Ertak's. It had also been a little like Dr. Chase-Huebner's, though in reality, he recalled, these two had never sounded in the least alike.

Jorn spread his hands helplessly.

"Whoever it is, they're sick," he said. "We'd better get in fast. Resume drilling."

"Arrchk. Arr hamds. Rk."

The cherry-red half-disc of metal canted suddenly, and then fell on the other side of the door. The boy put the cutter down carefully and yanked the two unlocked dogs free, pushing open the door and walking through it without waiting for orders.

Then he put his hand over his mouth and tried to get out again, but he could not entirely battle the press of people pushing after him; somehow the word had been passed, and the control barrel was almost crowded now. He was sick in their midst before he could break free into the barrel itself. The rest sidled slowly into the cabin along the walls, less because they wanted to than because the pressure of people behind them made it imperative.

It was wholly incredible. Certainly the youngsters could not have understood it; though they could clearly see that it was horrible, they could hardly begin to guess where the real horror lay. They lacked the data for any such awareness.

At first glance, Jorn thought that the wizened old lady was still alive. It was only long minutes later, at third or fourth look, that he saw that the open eyes were dull and unwinking, and that she was in fact almost mummified. She was seated on the deck, leaning against the hull, her mouth sagging open on one side.

Ertak, nude except for a few scraps, lay on his bunk, looking even smaller than the woman. His great shoulders and chest had somehow vanished; in death it could be seen that his frame had in fact been perfectly normal for his height and weight. He too looked quite dried out, so that it was impossible to guess how long he had been dead; but appearance alone both of them might have been lying there for months, though their "cabin boy" had spoken to one of them—he did not know which—through the door only two days ago.

But all this was secondary to the central terror. In the middle of the deck there lay coiled the serpentine shape of a familiar so huge that Jorn did not at first even recognize it for what it was. Its head was as big as a large book ... and as the invaders tried to press back against the inward urging of the curious people outside, it raised that head from the floor.

"Rrch," it said, in a hoarse feminine parody of Ertak's voice. "Rk. Arr hamds. Tsu arr hamds."

At the very center of its coils, in the geometric center of the cabin, there rested a smooth, dully shining sphere, about the size and shape, and even almost the color, of an apple.

"Out," Jorn croaked. "Everybody out. Who's Sergeant Strage's successor? Never mind yet—out, quick!"

The familiar watched them go, her head weaving back and forth slightly. Jorn was the last one; and with more courage than he had ever dreamed he possessed, he stopped on the sill to look around the cabin for the Grand Log.

If it was still there, it was nowhere in sight. Then he found himself looking first into the eyes of the mummified woman, and then into the eyes of the familiar.

"Yerrow Warming Ome," the voice rasped. "Arr hamds. Arr hands."

He fled, and the bulkhead was secured behind him by willing, shaking hands.

"Great Ghost," someone quavered. "What ... what *is* that?"

He did not answer for a few minutes. He could not have spoken had he wanted to.

"The armorer," he croaked at last.

"That's Prin Tober," Kasi said in a hushed voice. "I've called her, Father."

"Call her again. Tell her to bring a flame-thrower."

"Jorn—" Ailiss said hesitantly.

"Yes. Now it's up to you, Ailiss."

"No, no, I—I just wanted to ask a question. Why me?"

"Because you're in command now. Ertak's dead, the doctor's dead, the stand-by captain died on Salt Flats, Kamblin's dead. That leaves you."

"Absolutely not," Ailiss said, sounding a little surer of herself. "I relinquish it, formally and officially. I will *not* be in command over my own husband—not at my age."

"Well," Jorn said drily, "since I'm the last other officer, I'm getting at least one order from you: *Take over*. All right. Where's that girl?"

"Here, Director," a voice at his right said. He was still too deeply in shock to take more than marginal notice of the title. He was a little too old now to be tickled by such gauds, anyhow. He was even less able to notice how completely, in only half a century, the last faint traces of the Matriarchy had vanished.

He looked the girl over, bearing in mind that she had not seen what still awaited them inside the Director's cabin. She was sturdy, flat-footed, straight-haired, and her gaze was direct and matter-of-fact; very much like his first memory of Sergeant Strage, in fact, though, of course, much younger. She held the flame-thrower as though she knew how to use it. He decided that she would do.

He walked to his desk, unlocked a drawer, and retrieved his side-arm, checking it as he returned to the enigmatic and fatal door. It had been a long time since he had even worn it, let alone used it, but it seemed to be all right. It was armed, and would fire.

"A couple of the boys are going to undog that bulkhead for you," he told the youthful armorer. "As soon as it swings open, and you're sure that the boys are in the clear, I want you to cut loose. No matter what you see, no matter *what*, burn that room out. I'll be right behind you, covering you. Understand?"

"Yes, Director. All ready." She planted her feet, standing directly in front of the cabin, her tanks of fuel and propellant hunched high on her sturdy back, the flame-thrower canted slightly downward in her gloved hands, her mask pulled down over her face.

"All right." Jorn drew a deep breath. "Open up."

The dogs fell and the door swung inward. Jorn had only the briefest of glimpses inside, but it was more than he wanted.

"Rk. Yerrow Warming—"

The flame-thrower gushed inferno. Despite his promise, Jorn had to fall back immediately, his eyes streaming. The girl stood where she was, an immobile form of solid black framed in a panel of intolerable bright yellow glare.

Inside the cabin there was a single high-pitched squeak, like the pinch of air escaping from a balloon; and then, a small, muffled detonation. The curtain of yellow fire seemed to ripple, and the armorer took one step back.

The flame-thrower died out with a sputter of black smoke. Everyone was coughing. The aperture to the hell that had been the cabin glowed cherry, then crimson, and finally went black, but waves of heat continued to whelm out from it. The girl pushed up her mask.

"Cleaned out, Director."

"Thank you," Jorn said, swallowing hard. "Well done. Very well done." He could think of nothing more adequate to say. She must have looked for at least a second into that room, and into those eyes; but she had not even quivered.

"Nothing to it," she said, shaking a last little spatter of fire-drops from the nozzle of the flame-thrower onto the deck. "I'm glad I finally got to use it for something."

She marched out, disconnecting her hoses as she went. Jorn wondered crazily: has she no curiosity at all? But Sergeant Strage wouldn't have had, either.

"What's next?" Monel said. He seemed, to Jorn's secret and malicious pleasure, to be a little dazed.

"We've got a Yellow Warning," he said. "Pull the tapes and look them over. That's your job, isn't it? When you've got a digest of what's on them, report to me in my cabin—no later than tomorrow noon."

"The tapes? Oh, of course. Yes, all right."

"No, it's not all right. Try again."

The youngster looked up, startled, into his father-in-law's eyes. Then his expression turned slightly sullen.

"Yes, Director."

Unfortunately, Kasi chose this moment to giggle. That was not going to improve matters. All the same,

Jorn enjoyed it. His small streak of sadism was one of his few remaining pleasures.

"Ailiss, let's go." Heads high, the Director and his consort walked arthritically out of the control barrel.

"Now, Director," Ailiss said sardonically over the Castles board, "tell me what you make of that affair, or I won't make another move, double jeopardy or no double jeopardy."

"I'd make more of it if I knew more about synthetic biochemistry," Jorn said reluctantly. "I never saw a familiar that size before and I didn't know it was possible. But Ertak was old and he never married, so I suppose he had the sheer time for it—though he must have pampered her beyond belief, enough to make him quite sick now and then."

"I knew that much," Ailiss said. "It was his own special vice. There are a few other cases in the literature, though none of them are this extreme. His mother tried to—"

"His *mother?*"

"Yes. Dr. Chase-Huebner. He was a reject of the Chase line. That's how he got her into The Project; she felt guilty at having made Jon Huebner such a favorite, and a partner in her cancer research and so on, and having dumped her earlier son. When Ertak got to be an eminent scientist in his own right, he had a club he could use, and he did."

Jorn stared at his wife with new eyes. "And you knew this all the time?"

"Well, ever since she tried to persuade him to give up the familiar before take-off. She couldn't make him; she was afraid to try. Otherwise, you'd have had to give up Tabath, and the same for all the other bachelors."

"Great Ghost. Hmm. How many of them are there aboard ship now, do you think?"

"None, I'm almost sure," Ailiss said. "Everyone surviving from the first generation is married; and of course, we couldn't make new familiars for the male children, we didn't have the laboratory to reproduce them." The wrinkles at the corners of her eyes suddenly deepened sharply. "Though from what I saw back up there, she'd solved that problem. Quite an achievement, when you look at it dispassionately."

"Yes. An egg. That's what I took that apple-thing to be, too. But only on intuition." He stared down at the still-incomplete game on the Castles board. "And *you* were asking *me* what I thought of all this! You might as well go on. Why did she do it?"

"Do what?"

"Don't dodge, Ailiss, this is your field. Why did she help her son's familiar to make the egg?"

"If I told you that you would go out of your own mind."

"There seem to be a good many things that you don't tell," he said stiffly.

"There are some things I don't tell until I'm asked," she said, "and some I don't tell even then. You want an explanation? It depends on who died first. We'll never know that now, and we might never have been able to figure it out; obviously the familiar was living off the corpses' body fluids, which was a new departure in itself. But if *he* died first, then she knew the familiar would die soon after unless she could get it to reproduce; strong though it was, it needed some new emotional attachment. And she still felt that she owed him something. So ... I suppose you could say that the egg was her grandchild."

Jorn choked, nearly upsetting the board.

"You see?" Ailiss said. "Where would it get me,

peddling that kind of information to anybody who asked for it? The first thing a psychologist learns is to keep her mouth shut around laymen." She reached out and picked up a charger, twiddled it judiciously, and moved it from *here* to *there.*

"I can see why ... She must have been crazy, poor old woman. You know, I almost loved her once, old though she was even when we met."

"Of course, I know," Ailiss said. "And if it comforts you any, she wasn't crazy at all. She was being quite normal. I haven't given you the real explanation, and I don't plan to, either ... All right, that's my move; and now *you're* in jeopardy, Director."

There was a decorous knock at the door of their cabin. It was divinely well timed, from Jorn's point of view; though he spent the rest of his life wondering what he would have said next, nothing satisfactory ever occurred to him.

The knocker was Monel. He was being very stiff and formal.

"The tapes, Director."

"Very good," Jorn said, trying to regroup some of the scraps of his dignity. "Report."

"It's a yellow dwarf star, sir, forty-one hundred light years from our point of origin; surface temperature about fifty-five hundred degrees. The computer says ten planets, possibly eleven. No evidence of patterned electromagnetic activity. The star is third generation and good for about five thousand million years more at a minimum before it begins to expand."

"Hmm. Pretty cold star. Anything else?"

"Very little as yet, sir," the boy said stiffly. "Except that the star is a double."

"A double? With *planets?*"

"Yes, Director. There's a small white dwarf located

about half a light year below the south pole of the yellow sun, and their masses are such that at that distance they have to be in orbit around each other. It's almost a duplicate of the doublet system we passed at extreme range just a few weeks ago. But the larger star here has planets; we can even see the biggest one from here, just barely."

"I see. Very good. Dismissed."

"Thank you, sir. Uhm . . . Director?"

"What is it?"

"Do you have any further orders, sir?"

Jorn frowned. He did not; that was his trouble. It was, of course, remotely possible that the lonely and decrepit *Javelin* had finally found herself a stop, but it was not very likely—surely not in a system as outré as this one. One more Yellow Warning like this and he would be convinced for good and all that the computer, like the one the black men had devised and entrusted their fate to, was deranged; none of its choices, now that he came to think of it, had ever been very close to the model it was supposed to have been set to scan for.

And did they really *want* a stop? Now, after all this time? They were in no shape to fight for a planet, not only with hostile natives, but even with blind nature. It would be so much easier simply to glide onward forever. Now that they could be sure that they were not likely to run head-on into the dangers and mysteries of the galactic center, they might continue to go uneventfully along parallel to the rim until death solved their problems, and no longer have to cope at all with their old, foolish notions of having had some definite, Elysian goal.

Why not? With Ertak dead, it was suddenly easy to see that the armada itself had never been more than a daydream, a minute and evanescent soap-bubble in the eternal silver-and-black silences of the sidereal universe.

"Maintain course," Jorn said. "No further orders at present."

The boy left. Jorn turned back to the board with a sigh to consider his next move. He was aware of Ailiss' eyes upon him, but he did not look up.

He had had enough for one day—or one lifetime. More than enough.

14

But, as he knew well enough in his heart of hearts, he had finally to make up his mind. When he came into the control barrel with Ailiss, almost all the young officers were already gathered, watchful and waiting. Feeling utterly displaced, he mounted the bridge, and after a while was able to bring himself to sit down in Ertak's old chair ... though not without a shudder. Before him was the master screen, with a tiny yellow globe shining, like a lambent egg, in its geometric center.

"Very well, posts, everyone. Monel, report, please."

"Director, we have continued on course as you ordered. This has brought us well inside one light year of the system."

Jorn repressed a start. He should have checked that before issuing any orders; but what was done was done. "Go on."

"This is a ten-planet system; the presumptive eleventh is actually an asteroid belt between planets four and five. Number five is the gas giant first spotted by the computer; it is large but not as large as the one recorded for system IEP number three. Six, seven, eight and ten are also gas giants of moderate size. Nine is a small dense world about eight thousand miles in diameter with a very eccentric orbit; presumably it is an escaped satellite of number eight, which also has four other moons, all much smaller. Number ten has two moons, and number seven has five. Number six has twelve, including a large one, plus a small asteroid belt of its own, which the spectroscope shows to be mostly ice. Number five has fourteen satellites, three of them large. None of these bodies are livable. Then comes the asteroid belt, followed by four small dense planets, two of which appear to be inhabitable."

"Two of them? Around so cold a star?"

"Yes, Director. Number four is small and cold and wouldn't support us except under domes, but it shows traces of water and indigenous simple plant life. Number three is a binary, consisting of one planet about two thousand miles in diameter and one of about eight thousand miles, revolving around each other. The smaller body is quite dead and meteor-battered, and obviously never had any atmosphere to speak of. The larger is almost an exact duplicate of our home world in many important respects, according to the computer, except that it has much more extensive bodies of water. The land areas show a few limited deserts, but for the most part are completely covered with plant life, apparently very complex. This binary system is at a mean distance from the primary of about ninety-three million miles. The two innermost planets are not inhabitable."

As close as that? Jorn thought. *That's no good. One really extensive solar flare, and—*

But life took a long time to arise. Evidently there hadn't been any solar flare big enough to be dangerous for some 500 million years, at the least.

"How quiet is the star, Monel?"

"Very quiet, Director. It's a micro-variable. Judging by spot types, the longest period would seem to be about ten years. During that time the solar constant may vary by about two per cent—certainly no more."

"I see. What is the situation in the binary system itself? The dynamical situation?"

"Stable, Director. The two worlds are about a quarter of a million miles apart, and separating slowly, because of tides in the oceans I mentioned. The tidal friction appears as an increase in the angular momentum of the smaller planet; but it's very slight."

There went another possible out. Jorn sighed.

"Recommendations?"

There was a long silence. Finally he realized that they were waiting for him to turn around. When he did so, Monel's hand was raised.

"Go ahead, Monel."

"Director, we know that this isn't exactly the kind of star that the computer is supposed to favor. But we ask leave to remind you that our generation can't share your prejudices in the matter, or the computer's either. We have never seen a blue-white super-giant star except in pictures—and in one of those pictures, we saw it blow up. If this little yellow star has a livable planet, we think we ought to try it. There's— there's something to be said for a star that's good for another five thousand million years."

Quite so, Jorn thought, reading the tone as well as the words. And though you are far from being as excited as we would have been, at your age, about making another planet-fall, still you're contemptuous of our laxness; and convinced that whatever this planet-fall may turn out to involve, you'll make a better job of it than we would have.

And you ought to have the chance. What can it

matter to the rest of us now, the tiny remnant? One death is as good as another, if death is what you are courting.

And after Ertak, it was clear that almost anything was better than dying in bed.

"Very good," he said. "I agree. We will sit down."

And then he had to grin as he watched the boy's tense belligerence sag sidewise into surprise.

The continents passed across the master screen, and then were replaced, again and again, by enormous oceans. There was a *lot* of water here, for sure.

There were also several inarguable cities. Jorn studied the photographs anxiously, despite his inner resignation; but the towns were uniformly mud-brick affairs, each structure heaped squatly into a pyramid, with the levels connected by ramps. Beyond the ziggurats were slums, and beyond these, enormous acres of tilled fields; it looked as though as many as five acres were required to feed each and every person in one of these little nations.

The cities were also isolated. The rest of this world was pure jungle. That there was a sort of civilization arising here could not be argued, but it was obviously primitive, based upon the most back-breaking, around-the-clock labor—slave labor, almost beyond question. So it appeared to Jorn.

An almost microscopically close examination of the giant moon had showed nothing. It was dead, and always had been. The fourth planet, on the other hand, still had rudimentary vegetation; but its surface was cracked and split and tilted like a vast artillery target by millennia, even by geological ages of bombardment by large strays from this system's asteroid belt. If it had ever held advanced forms of life— which was in itself very doubtful, considering the planet's small size—they had been bombed out by more planet-wide concussions than an aching old head cared to visualize. There was nothing to fear from that direction.

"We'll be touching down after the next circuit, Director. Near the spur of the large southern continent that's shaped like a big upside-down buskin."

"I see no objection. Let her go, Monel. I think this is it."

"Yes, sir!"

The *Javelin* creaked, righted herself, and glided down like a dowager, dignified, ancient, and more than a little weary. The green world rushed up to meet her.

She settled. The engines throbbed once and were silent. Was it over at last—or, once more, just beginning?

Silence.

"Orders, Director?"

Jorn got painfully up out of the Director's chair. He had never been comfortable in it.

"Prepare your disembarkation party."

"But . . . Tests, Director?"

"The party will be your test," Jorn said, making his way down the stairway from the bridge to the floor of the control barrel. "We have nobody to man the laboratories any more; what we need now are guinea-pigs. I'll go first; and if something happens . . . Ailiss? What is it?"

"A point of privilege, Director," Jorn's wife said steadily. "I am as entitled to be first out as you are. And then if something happens, all the original crew will be gone, and the children will be in charge. That's *their* privilege, Director."

Jorn could feel the tears coming. He choked them back as best he could; but he was old . . . old.

"I was going to ask you," he said, not ashamed—no, not really—of the quaver in his voice. "But I didn't quite know how... Monel, put out a crane, and rig us some kind of cab. I'm afraid we won't be able to manage the ladder."

They had meant to come back to the *Javelin*: Jorn was always positive about that. But after walking carefully a while, hand in hand, in the singing, flower-burdened heat, with the heart-stopping blue sky bending above them, they came to a yellow, rutted road.

There was a man trudging along it, blue-bearded and bronze-skinned. Behind him he was leading a four-legged animal, gray, with a long mournful face and long mobile ears, and with a net thrown across its back in which earthenware jugs and bolts of cloth were entwined. It had a long slim tail with a tassel, with which it switched incessantly at small insects which harried it, in absurdly familiar fashion.

The man was dressed in skirts of some skin with the wool still on it; the wool had been twisted into little decorative tufts. Some part of his clothing, also, was metal, but it did not seem to be armor, but merely ceremonial—otherwise he would have shucked it off in the heat. He looked at them, and at their clothing, without any apparent surprise.

He was wholly human. That did not surprise Jorn either. There was, he had come to suspect, a Model.

Jorn asked the greeting question. The man only nodded, and pointed down the road, the way he had been going.

"Gerzea," he said, and beckoned. He tugged at the sad little animal. Jorn and Ailiss, wondering, each grasped a hand in the netting, and followed.

It was a long journey. The man was kind in his brutal way, but they were old. He buried them in the sands not far west of the Faiyum, and resumed his pilgrimage; and it may be also that he forgot them.

But they had come, with all the rest of the civilized world of 3900 B.C., to within miles of the crowning of the Earth's first king.

epilogue

It is written:
That given any one of a thousand million possible paths, life will take them all;

That worlds which will support life will give birth to it;

That worlds which cannot support intelligent life will be colonized;

And that where both can take place, both will take place.

It is written that this is what the vast, unknowing interstellar stage is for: To be given consciousness and purpose while its gift of existence lasts.

It is written:
That this is a random process;

That in the end all will be darkness and silence again;

But that while it lasts, life spreads through it, to make it aware of its own vastness and beauty, which otherwise it can never have known.

This is a gift; but the Giver is unknown.

That too is written.

1086 A.D.: A sudden glare of light in the constellation later called Taurus. The Chinese astronomer T'ang Yaou-Shun marks it down: *A new and marvelous star, portending miracles.*

But the miracle has already happened. It sleeps inside Yaou-Shun, in twelve of his genes.

SUPERIOR
FANTASY AND SCIENCE FICTION
FROM AVON BOOKS